BUT FOR THE CRASH

George A.M. Heroux

Victim Impact Speakers

Copyright © 2012, Second Edition

All rights reserved – George A.M. Heroux

No part of this book may be reproduced or transmitted in any form or by any means, graphic, electronic, or mechanical, including photocopying, recording, taping, or by any information storage retrieval system, without the permission, in writing, from the publisher.

Victim Impact Speakers
4030 Thornbrook Drive
Springfield, IL 6271
www.victimimpactspeakers.com

ISBN: 978-1-60911-453-4

Printed in the United States of America

Chapter One

Patti had long ago acclimated to the brisk Minnesota chill that would send most students her age to the warmth of a shelter. She thrived in this weather even though her native Illinois seldom foisted such iciness on its citizens, at least not for a prolonged period. Just like some residents of the Dakotas or perhaps sections of Wisconsin, and of course Alaska, Minnesotans seemed to adore frosty air. Sturdy folks. As a sophomore at Howard Christian College, Patti had grown to love this weather for reasons that only inhabitants of Minnesota understand.

  A small travel bag sat on the hard ground beside her. The trip was to be for one week only, and she was assured that laundry facilities would be available. She had no need for dress clothes or party dresses. Her trip was to provide two hands to a church's reconstruction project in New Orleans. She bent slightly and picked up the bag as a car slowed and stopped in front of her.

  "Hey, Patti," the driver hollered into the murky air. "Rarin' to go?"

  "Get in," the woman in the passenger seat said. "It's cold out there. We're picking up Heather at her dorm."

  There was excitement in the cold air. It all started when a notice was posted in the student recreation room. It was a plea for help. A very popular church was in dire need of a week's worth of labor – painting, patching, cleaning, and fixing. The church sent an SOS to Howard Christian College and a few other selected schools for some free labor. Perhaps there were students who would donate their spring vacation to this effort in lieu of a week on a beach somewhere. To these students leaving the college today for a week, this sounded like an opportunity to have some camaraderie and to give something of themselves. Only the students of a college with Howard Christian's ideals would be likely to respond to such a request.

Walter Caine was the finance manager for the largest car dealer in Springfield, Foster Ford. It had been a remarkably successful month. Only a few more closed deals by this very aggressive sales team would break the record for April and exceed sales quotas for the month by a wide margin, a reason to celebrate.

"Going with us tonight?" The question came from Paul Preston, Foster Ford's top salesman for the month.

"I guess. This is the first beat-the-quota month of the year. I have to give you guys all the encouragement I can."

Paul shrugged. "Wouldn't be the same without you, Buddy. Want me to drive?"

Walter shook his head. "Naw, I have a company car for the weekend. I'll drive myself and go home from there. Where we going?"

"We gave that a lot of thought," Paul said. "Friday's. That's the happening place. We'll be there about seven."

"Sounds good, Amigo," Walter shouted as Paul quickly left the finance manager's office – a prospective customer was coming through the front door.

Paul demonstrated exactly why he was salesman of the month. He showed the customer what the customer wanted to see, then he showed the customer what he wanted him to see. This bit of sleight of hand ended with the customer's signature on the dotted line. That was the deal that put Foster Ford over the top for the biggest April ever. Now, if only the customer can somehow afford the more expensive car that became his object of desire through Paul's subtle direction. Walter found a way. The company worked with several banks and had a variety of payment packages. Within twenty minutes, Walter had found financing that would work for the company and for the customer.

Cayla was still in the driver's seat as her car, with passengers Patti, Maris, and Heather, moved along the highway past Eau Claire, Wisconsin. "Everybody up for some driving? I figure it will be about four hours each. Piece of cake."

"Especially since we get to take a rest break in the middle of the night at Patti's parents in Collinsville," Heather pointed out. "Are you sure we're welcome at that time of night?"

"Sure. We should be good for an early breakfast, too," Patti said.

Patti hadn't seen her parents since the Christmas break. She was an only child who adored her parents not only because they were financing her education but because her parents were kind, energetic, intelligent, and loving. Asking her mother to whip up a breakfast for four hungry students was tantamount to asking her to open a door. No, it was better than that because her mother was anxious to perform this small favor. She and her husband were looking forward to meeting the other students. They knew that her friends would be the kind of girls who would be personable, bright, and pleasant – mirror images of their daughter Patti.

It wasn't long after Patti left for school that her parents realized how much they would miss the perky and pretty Patti, a phrase occasionally used by her father. The fact that she was attractive did not go unnoticed by the boys in her high school, but Patti was much too popular to concern herself with any one boy. At college, her outgoing personality resulted in considerable attention also but now from boys who were more serious, studious, and ambitious. However, she continued to leave her options open.

Friday's was happening. Walter and Paul entered at the same time, seven on the clock.

"There they are," Paul said, gesturing toward a large table where five men and two women were already seated.

"Party time," was the greeting from one of the women. "We're drinking Zombies. We have a pitcher just for you guys."

Paul picked up the pitcher and poured a drink for Walter and then for himself. "Here's to our leader," gesturing toward Walter.

Walter held his glass up. "Heck, all I do is make sure your deals get financed. Your group can flat-out sell. Here's looking at the best damn sales team in the state, maybe in the country."

Jerry, one of the men in the group, shouted over to Walter. "Hey, Wally. How did a baby face like you ever get to be finance manager anyway?"

Ruth, the woman who had shouted the welcome to them, jumped in: "He has a baby face 'cause he's a baby. How old are you, Sweetheart?"

"I'm twenty-eight going on about sixty in this job. I won't ask you your age, though, Ruth. If nothing else, I am a gentleman."

Jack, another man in the group, held up his glass: "Are we here to drink or to talk work like old ladies?"

"We're drinking because of work, Dummy," Paul said.

"We haven't drunk enough to entitle you to call me Dummy, Lamebrain."

"Objection overruled," Paul responded. "Now is it time for a good ole-fashioned drinking game or not?"

It's odd that alcohol turns full-grown adults into children or at best teenagers, not physically of course, but the part of the brain that produces common sense goes on vacation. It didn't matter whether the game was created on the spot or was as old as Roman toga parties. The end result was the same: bottoms up. This group was there to celebrate and celebrate is what they did – all of them. Nowhere in sight was a designated driver.

Now, Heather was the driver, and Patti was in the passenger seat providing stay-awake conversation. Cayla and Maris, who had completed their driving shifts, were sound asleep in the backseat.

"Ever been to Springfield?" Patti asked. "It's about an hour and a half down the road."

"Nope," Heather answered. "Actually, I would love to visit sometime. I'm a bit of a Lincoln buff."

"I lived eighty miles from Springfield all of my life. I visited with my family a few times, and my senior class in high school came here to roam the Lincoln sites."

"There's a Presidential museum there now. That's completed, isn't it?"

"Sure," Patti said. "I was in Springfield last year during the summer. My parents couldn't wait to see it."

"Your parents are saints to put up with an early morning visit from four college girls," Heather observed.

"Oh, they'll love having us, even if we're only going to stay for an hour or so."

"Your dad's a minister, isn't he?" Heather asked.

"Yes, but he has a problem, Parkinson's disease. He's pretty much had to retire."

"That's sad. But, you know, I read somewhere that people with P.D. can still live a long time. Isn't Cayla's father a minister, too?" Heather asked.

Patti smiled. "Yes, he is. He's the only divorced minister I know. But her mother may be more interesting: She's the CEO of a really major corporation. I forget which one."

"Really? That's great, really great – the CEO thing, I mean, not the divorce thing."

"How about you?" Patti asked. "You have a minister for a parent?"

"No, not me. My folks aren't thrilled all that much that I'm at a Christian college. Don't get me wrong. They're great parents. They're just not religious."

"Then, how could you have…"

Heather interrupted: "I'm an independent thinker. Sometimes parents are wrong, that's all."

"Anyway," Patti said, "We're not going to see much of Springfield. The highway just curves around it."

Patti was accurate in her description of the highway that avoids downtown Springfield. The four-lane road is both Route 72 that goes east and west and Route 55 that goes north and south. These two highways join for the move around the city of Springfield to the east and then part after leaving the main section of the city. Curving around Springfield was not an exact description, however. There is only one area on the joined highway that constitutes a slanting curve where a driver can not see the highway ahead for several miles.

Paul and Walter staggered out of the bar, hanging on to each other. The celebration had gone on for more than three hours.

"There's the old company car, Wally," Paul said. "You gonna be able to drive all right, fella?"

"Yeah, I'm fine. I might take a little nap before I hit the road."

"You live in Decatur, don't you?"

"It's about a forty minute drive. Do it twice a day."

Paul opened the car door for Walter and eased him in behind the wheel. "Okay, Wally, ole pal. Drive carefully."

Paul, quite inebriated himself, was not in any condition to advise Walter to drive carefully. If he had been sober and responsible, he would have discouraged Walter from getting into that car that evening to the point of taking his keys away from him. Alas, Paul was neither sober nor responsible. This night, he was not Walter's friend, because friends don't let their friends drive drunk.

It was almost midnight when the car with four Howard Christian College students approached Springfield. Heather was still in the driver's seat. Patti had been nodding off but was now alert.

"I can take over anytime you want," Patti said. "I'll cruise us into Collinsville."

"Why not?" Heather answered. "Let's switch at a rest stop or a McDonald's. Either of those coming up, do you remember?"

Patti thought a minute. "I think there might be a few Mickey Ds in the exits ahead."

"Okay, I'll watch for one," Heather said.

Since Heather wasn't really tired at this point, she wasn't really anxious to give up the wheel. She was rather enjoying the drive, reminding her of the trips she made to other vacation spots when she was younger and when her parents allowed her to drive for the first time on a highway very similar to this one. She knew also that there had to be a McDonald's at every one of these exits. Maybe she would just drive on to the next rest stop.

Walter rested uncomfortably with his head against the side window, then woke with a start and mumbled out loud to himself: "I'm dead. Let's go home, Wally, and rest on a real pillow." He started the engine and moved slowly out of the parking lot. He steered his car onto a four-line road. A sign read 72 West, then 72 East next right. "Why do they have to make this so complicated?" he asked himself. There was no car in front or in back of him when he turned onto the exit, not the entrance, of Route 72, even though a bright red and white sign shouted WRONG WAY. Within a few seconds, he was on the highway and increasing his speed up to and past the sixty-five mile speed limit.

By the time the students reached the slight curve on 55/72, all four of them were awake albeit drowsy. There was an audible gasp, a scream of "look out," a mumbled groan as all four of the students saw a car headed directly toward them, driving on the wrong side of the highway. In the other car, Walter's heart sank; in that instant, and not before then, he realized what he had done.

The crash was explosive, the results horrendous. Meeting head-on, both cars weighing over 2,000 pounds and traveling at speeds in excess of 65 miles an hour, in an instant there were torn steel and ripped bodies distributed randomly on the highway.

No study has ever determined how or why some people survive such a crash. The angle of impact to individual bodies? The amount of steel directly fortifying to some extent any one individual? The work of God, one person's mission on earth not completed? Just luck? Whatever the reason, Patti, Maris, and Cayla died in that moment. Heather suffered fourteen broken bones and numerous lacerations. Walter broke his arm, that's all.

While time was no longer relevant for three Howard Christian College students, time stood still for Heather and Walter. The wrecked cars smoldered. The smell of burned seatbelts and torn steel punctured the air. A passer-by stopped and called 911 on his cell phone. Almost immediately, wailing sirens pierced the formerly quiet night. Within moments, one and then several other State Police vehicles were at the scene, quickly followed by emergency medical technicians. Later, that first State Policeman to arrive at the site of the crash pronounced this collision as the worst he had seen in his twenty years as a police officer. The image would stay with him for the rest of his life.

Chapter Two

A few hours later, a State Policeman arrived at Mary and Bill Goodwin's front door. They had received a call about a half-hour earlier. They had been told that Patti had been in an accident and that someone would be contacting them as soon as possible with an update on Patti's condition. They feared the worst. Their fears were realized in the person of State Policeman Ed Collins at the door. Sergeant Collins was invited in, and Bill and Mary sat down. Instantly, they both knew they were about to get news that they couldn't hear while standing.

There are a number of individuals who are trained in notification – the art, I suppose, of telling family members about the death of a loved one. It is not an easy task. The job falls to police officers, doctors, or coroners mostly. It is traumatic enough to lose a member of the family without having the news being given in a phone call or through some other stark, sudden communication. Typically, family members are told by phone that there has been an accident and that they should go to the hospital as soon as possible. The accident victim may have been killed instantly in the crash, but that news, nevertheless, is withheld until someone trained in notification can accomplish that unenviable communications task.

"We've been asked by our Springfield District office to give you some sad news about your daughter Patti," Trooper Collins said. "I'm sorry to be the bearer of such news, but Patti has lost her life in a car crash in Springfield. I'm so sorry."

Bill, already in almost constant pain from his Parkinson's, moaned softly. "Are you sure?" Bill asked. "You know there were four girls in the car. They were supposed to be here during the night. Are you sure it was Patti? Are you certain?"

"Tragically, three of the girls died in the crash. Only one survived. Heather Sanford is in serious condition in Memorial Hospital in Springfield."

Mary, as always in any critical situation, was the practical thinker. "What should we do? Should we go to Springfield?"

"Our coroner will be in touch with you later today. She'll explain what she'll need from you," Sergeant Collins said.

"What do you know about what happened?" Mary asked. "Were they struck by another vehicle?"

"Yes, there was another car involved, a drunk driver, we believe, driving on the wrong side of the highway. That's about all I know at this point. I'm sure you'll get a call shortly and that, eventually, you'll be informed of all the details."

"I'm sorry," Mary said. "Can I get you a cup of coffee or something? I'm not thinking very clearly."

"No, no, thank you, Mrs. Goodwin," the Trooper said, moving slowly to the door. "Again, I'm sorry."

It wasn't until the door closed that tears flowed from the eyes of both Mr. and Mrs. Goodwin. The official notification made it all real – their daughter was dead. Bill tried to comfort Mary by sitting next to her on the sofa with his arm around her, but it was Bill who was inconsolable in his sorrow.

"How could this have happened to our little Patti," he said. "We always protected her. Why couldn't we have protected her this time?"

Suddenly, Mary felt totally inadequate. She had been the strong one, coaxing Bill not to give up in dealing with his Parkinson's. She had the ramp built, encouraged him to learn all he could about the disease, helped him to form a support group, was by his side for stability and comfort. Even as a child, Mary, the eldest child of six children, was the go-to of the family, not only for her siblings but for a mother who struggled with mental illness. Mary saw to it that brothers and sisters pursued educational opportunities vigorously. Her own education was completed with an M.A. in Nursing that proved to serve Bill well as the disease progressed now too rapidly. But now what?

Bill Goodwin had always been a quiet man whose primary goal was to serve. He did so magnificently, providing moral sustenance to his flock at First Congregational Church for over twenty years. No one was more respected in the church community. Parkinson's disease came suddenly and unexpectedly when he noticed a slight tremor, at that time totally unexplained. Then came a failure of reflexes leading to an impaired balance and falls. It was not difficult for his general physician to recognize these cardinal symptoms. It had been four years since the diagnosis. Now, in addition to the motor aspects, his speech had become soft, hoarse, and monotonous.

"We need to be strong, Bill," Mary said quietly. "Strong and brave. We have to face the horror in front of us – the funeral, the legal matters – in a way that would make Patti proud of us."

"Yes, I know," Bill replied softly. "I'll try, but it will be very difficult. First, I have to deal with why the God we espoused, that we revered, would let this happen to us. So many times, others have told me exactly that, and now I am expressing the same feelings."

When deaths occur and there needs to be someone to calm and advise the family, to see them through such a difficult period, it is very often the minister, the priest, or the rabbi who is up to the challenge. They know what to say and how to say it. This time, however, it was the minister who needed guidance. He needed to receive care and counsel, not dispense it.

Mary dropped to her knees. "Let us pray for Patti and her friends and then for us to have the strength to do whatever is needed of us, whatever our smart Patti would want us to do."

Paul and Ann Sanford were the parents of three girls, 28-year-old, now lawyer Elaine, 25-year-old newspaper reporter Carrie, and 20-year-old Heather, now lying seriously injured in Springfield's Memorial Hospital. Almost immediately after hearing the news of the crash, they made plans to travel from Cleveland, Ohio, to Springfield, Illinois.

"Were you able to get the plane and hotel reservations?" Ann asked.

"Yes," Paul answered. "I just got off the phone. We're leaving on United at 10:20."

"In the morning?"

"Of course in the morning," Paul said. "We're not flying out in the middle of the night."

"There's no need to bark at me," Ann responded. "I'm as worried about her as you are."

Paul shrugged and did not respond. Except for the enormous seriousness of the subject matter, this was not a particularly unusual conversation, or lack thereof, between Paul and Ann Sanford. Their relationship had been just fine in the early years, but all of that had changed fifteen years ago when Paul stepped outside of his marriage to find excitement and more satisfying companionship. The first affair lasted a year, and then there were others. Ann, who was always faithful in her marriage, never forgave him for those interludes although they had completely ceased in the last five years.

Paul was sixty years old. Ann had her fifty-eighth birthday the day after the crash. Obviously, there was no celebration. In fact, the birthday was not even noted; it was totally forgotten. Instead, all thoughts were with phone calls to family members and to the hospital, continued anguish concerning the crash, and plans for getting to Illinois as quickly as possible.

"Look," Ann continued, "we're going to spend a lot of time together in the next week or so. Let's try to be civil to each other."

"Please, Ann, can't we just think about Heather for the time being? If you hadn't agreed to have her go off to that Christian college, this would never have happened to her."

Ann picked up a book from the table and slammed it back on the table. "This is my fault? It's all my fault that Heather's in a hospital?"

"I didn't say that," Paul countered. "I'm just saying that we should never have agreed to have her go to school there. The first thing we're going to do when she's well is get her out of there."

"We agreed that she should go to college wherever she wanted. She picked Howard Christian. End of story."

"That college damn well almost killed her," Paul exploded. "That whole business of driving in the middle of the night for charitable labor. The school arranged that."

Ann was not in the mood to sooth Paul's temper tantrum. "Our daughter is still alive but may be in terrible pain. Can't we wait until she is well again before we start considering the school, her friends, everyone involved? Shouldn't our anger be with that drunk driver?"

"I have plenty of anger for him," Paul said. "I hope they put him away for the rest of his life. Even that's too good for him."

Chapter Three

The Sangamon County State's Attorney, John Blanchard, was new to this office having, four months ago, narrowly defeated a long-time incumbent who had been made vulnerable by an untidy, highly publicized spat with his wife that had ended in divorce. Blanchard had very little experience except for some criminal defense work in Chicago and as an administrator in the continuing legal education department of the American Bar Association. The latter job, however, gave him a broad knowledge of the law and the practice. He was young – only 32 – for the responsibility; Sangamon County was large with an unfortunate reputation of having several neighborhoods with constant criminal activity.

Usually, politicians who move into an area to run for office are not particularly welcomed or successful in their efforts. The State's Attorney position, however, may be unique in that a lawyer who can demonstrate some experience, knowledge, and energy is seen by the voters as one who is making a contribution to the county by making himself or herself available for the position. Blanchard liked the idea of moving away from the hubbub of Chicago to the relative serenity of downstate. Then, when he heard that the current occupant of the office was on shaky footing because of his personal life, Blanchard made the move to Springfield and announced his candidacy.

Even though Blanchard had competent, experienced prosecutors on his staff, he determined he would handle the case of the State v. Walter Caine. Certainly he would take advantage of the expertise of an Assistant State's Attorney or two, but he had determined that he was obligated to take on the important cases personally. Yes, the prosecution of a violent crime, drunk driving that resulted in three deaths and a serious injury, was very important to the community and to the young State's Attorney.

"Do you think we should oppose any motion for reduction of bond?" Blanchard asked. He was talking to long-time Assistant State's Attorney Garret Nelson.

"No," Nelson said. "I seriously doubt that there is a risk of flight. He'll still have to come up with $50,000 on a $500,000 bond. That's the likely amount. I understand that he owns a home. I suppose that he'll put that up for security."

"What do you hear about the condition of Heather Sanford?"

Nelson shook his head slowly. "She's in bad shape. She'll recover, they're saying, but the healing process is going to be long and arduous."

"If we have to go the trial, will she be able to testify, do you think?" Blanchard wondered.

"I don't know. She's going to be traumatized, I think, for a long time," Nelson said. "Anyway, John, I can't believe that this is going to trial."

"There won't be any plea negotiating in cases like this, not while I'm in this office."

Plea negotiating is an acceptable term and a practice often necessary to get a guilty plea. The term is far more acceptable to the phrase plea bargaining. In any case, it is the same practice of dropping one or some of several charges in order to get the defendant to plead guilty to one of the charges, sometimes the most serious. This guarantees a win without going to trial, leaving the uncertainties of a jury decision and unnecessary risks of losing at trial. However, when the plea negotiating results in dismissing the more serious charge in order to get a guilty plea on a lesser charge, there is always room for criticism. Then, it becomes quite obvious that the prosecutor may feel that it will be difficult to prove the greater charge so will settle for a guilty plea on the lesser charge to guarantee a conviction on something. That's when the hues and cries of victim family members and other observers are crescendo-like.

"I can't believe there will be a need for plea negotiation, John. I'll be surprised if we don't get a guilty plea. There's just no defense – he was drunk and he was driving on the wrong side of the road."

Blanchard thought a minute. "I'd like to get the families in here early. I want to assure them that we will not be plea bargaining and that we'll be going after the maximum sentence."

"We can set that up for sometime in the next few weeks, I think. Would you want our victim/witness coordinator to arrange that as soon as possible?"

"Absolutely," Blanchard said. "I want them and everyone in this county to understand that this office will not condone drunk driving deaths. We need to make an example of this defendant."

Norman Caswell has a strong stomach. Not everyone understood how he could have represented some of his clients. There was the hammer murderer, the guy who had his wife killed in a public parking garage, the serial rapist, and the man who killed his father for the inheritance money. It's true that defense lawyers will tell you that everyone charged with a serious crime is entitled to the best defense possible; that's clearly an integral part of the American judicial system. Norman always provided a spirited defense. That was his modus operandi; it reflected his professionalism: He provided the best defense he could muster, regardless of how he felt personally about the criminal or the criminal's deed.

Nevertheless, very personally, he felt an emotion deep in his gut when he provided his stellar defense. If, indeed, he was successful in his client's defense, that strong stomach was in some turmoil. Although praised for his acumen by fellow lawyers and, of course, by his clients, there was always that tinge of queasiness simultaneously present in those victories. Not that long before this date, he represented a drunk driver who seriously injured an elderly couple. While the court was in recess so that the judge could make a decision as to what extent the offender was to be punished, Norman made his way to the conference room that was occupied by the elderly couple. He apologized for the criminal conduct of his client and assured them that, in spite of his duty to defend his client, he knew that the man deserved any punishment that was to be dispensed by the judge and that, further, he hoped that the man would get a long sentence in prison.

And so it was that Norman Caswell had a churning, active stomach after he received a call asking that he defend Walter Caine against the charges of Aggravated DUI resulting in a death and Aggravated DUI resulting in great bodily harm. That was the terminology of the law. More precisely, it was three deaths and a serious injury. He looked across his desk, later that day, at Mr. and Mrs. Edward Caine.

"I'll do whatever I can to help you and your son," Norman said. "You know, though, that this is a very serious crime. In fact, it calls for a prison sentence of six to twenty-eight years if he is found guilty."

Ed and Betty Caine looked down as if they could avoid hearing the horrible truth if only they didn't make eye contact with the lawyer they were in the processing of hiring. After a moment, Ed said: "He never meant to hurt anyone. You know that, don't you?"

"It's a tough law, Mr. Caine," Norman said. "The way the law looks at it, he put people in danger when he drove a car while he was intoxicated. He meant to do that, so the law is based on that intention. The fact that some young people lost their lives was the consequence of that purposeful act of driving while impaired."

"But you'll make a jury understand that he didn't mean to kill anyone, won't you?" Mrs. Caine asked.

"Yes, but that might not help in these kinds of cases," Norman explained. "Anyway, we're getting ahead of ourselves. What we have to do first is have him plead not guilty at the arraignment. Then, we'll explore fully how I can best represent his interests."

"Do you mean that there might not be a trial?" Ed Caine asked.

"It's early for me to consider anything but preparing for a trial, but we may want to consider a guilty plea also. That's sometimes the best strategy to try to minimize any possible sentence."

"But there is a chance that he won't have to go to prison, isn't there?" Betty Caine asked. "Isn't it true that sometimes in these cases probation – is that what's it called? – that probation would be possible?" "That used to be the case, but the laws pertaining to drunk driving cases have gotten tougher. A few years ago, if there was a single death as a result of a drunk driving crash, the judge had to consider probation if the offender had no prior DUI arrests or no prior criminal record. That changed so that now the judge has to give prison time unless, the law now says, there are extraordinary circumstances that would require probation."

"What does that mean, extraordinary circumstances?" asked Ed Caine.

"We don't really know that. The law has been in effect for two years, and there has been no precedent established to define those words. In any case, under the new law or the old law, because there were multiple deaths, it is unlikely that the judge would consider probation. I'm sorry."

"Those poor people," Betty Cain said.

"Yes," Ed added. "Of course we're worried about our son, but the parents of those young people will never see their children again. It's terrible. Is there anything we should do? How can we apologize for what our son did?"

"Unfortunately, you really can't at this point," Norman said. "For the time being, Walter will be pleading not guilty. For now, it's really best that no admissions, no apologies are made. Maybe later, it will be possible to do that. For now, let me take the time to have a long conversation with Walter. I'll try to get him out on bail, but the bail may be high. I need to ask you if you and Walter have the money to meet bail and whether you have the money to pay for my services. That, unfortunately, is a basic necessity."

"I believe that Walter has some savings," Betty Caine said, "and he does own his own home, although I'm certain there's a large mortgage. Of course, we will help in any way we can. We have some savings also for Ed's retirement, but we've talked about it. If we have to spend everything we have to get the best legal representation for our son, we're willing to do that."

"Let's hope it doesn't come to that. Hopefully, Walter will provide the funds necessary. My secretary has prepared a document for you and one for Walter to retain me. Once we take care of that, I assure you that I'll do everything I can to provide the best possible representation for Walter."

Norman Caswell was to meet with Walter Caine that afternoon. He was not particularly looking forward to meeting with a man who was responsible for such a horrendous crash, one that killed three college students and injured a fourth. There was a small tinge in the hollow of his stomach.

Chapter Four

A very angry Paul Sanford stood outside of his daughter's hospital room. What he saw when he entered Heather's room was much worse than he expected. It is one thing to hear about broken bones and lacerations from 500 miles away. It was quite another thing to see the damages up close. He and Ann had just seen Heather for the first time since the crash. They had done all they could do to sooth Heather's pain by relating the positive report of the doctor and lying about her appearance. On the plus side, Heather was to be discharged in a matter of days although the road back to good health would be onerous at best.

Now, having said their temporary goodbyes, Paul could not take another step once he was outside of the range of Heather's hearing. "That son of a bitch. I'd like to get my hands on him for just five minutes."

"A lot of good that would do," Ann said. "He's twenty-eight. You're sixty. I think we should leave thoughts of revenge to the justice system."

"We know what the so-called justice system is like. Just last week, there was a drunk driver sentenced in Scranton, Pennsylvania. He ran off the road and killed his front-seat passenger. Then he tried to make it look like the passenger was the driver before the police arrived. He actually got out of the car, dragged the body of his passenger around, and put her behind the wheel. The police weren't that dumb; they were immediately suspicious. He finally admitted that he was the driver. You would think, with all of that, he would certainly go to prison. No, he got probation, thirty months of probation."

"We don't know all the circumstances, Paul," Ann said.

"Yeah, well, I do know that in the police reports, on the same day that that sentence was reported, a house burglar was given a three-year prison sentence and a hold-up guy was given six years in prison. That's justice?"

Again, justice takes what may be a fair rap. Criminal law penalties define the seriousness of the crime. Misdemeanors, for example, call for up to a year in the county jail. Felonies can send an offender to prison if the sentence is for more than a year. Specific sentences for specific crimes are dictated in laws enacted by legislatures. Since a great variety of laws emanate from the Legislature in different terms and over years, a more serious crime and then a harsher penalty varies with the hot button of the time the law is enacted. For example, if there is a much publicized and particularly tragic occurrence that catches the interest of a number of legislators, it is likely that they will join in an effort to prevent that act from happening again. Because feelings are running high at the time, and their effort is aimed at minimizing the reoccurrence of the act, the penalty in the new law may be extremely tough. In addition to that factor, as to what crimes should call for longer sentences is colored by what persons have been victimized by the crime. Subjectively, it is easy to say that one who causes a death – in any manner – should be punished more severely than one who, say, robs a bank and hurts no one. Nevertheless, the individuals who had to look down the barrel of the guns by threatening armed robbers, not knowing whether they were about to lose their lives, might feel that a severe sentence is quite appropriate for that deed. Bottom line, what is a fair sentence for one crime as opposed to another is the proverbial apples and oranges comparison.

"We have to get ourselves under control before we meet with the other parents," Ann said. "They've had a greater tragedy. They've lost their children forever."

"I'm concerned with all of our interests. When we meet with the State's Attorney tomorrow, he'd better have some answers."

Let us not forget the anguish during this time of the parents of Maris Oswald and the parents of Cayla Ferguson. Henry and Jessica Oswald were at their home in Oregon when they received the unwelcome news. Although Jessica had five daughters – no sons – Maris, a middle child, may have been the unannounced favorite. She was always upbeat and considerate of others, especially her mother. Jessica did not want Maris to leave for college, especially after Maris had selected a college a good distance from home.

Henry was an accountant by profession. Living in a world of numbers, it is not surprising that one of his initial thoughts after hearing about the crash was the improbability of his daughter losing her life in that way. After all, despite the significant toll of deaths on the highway, the odds were astronomical that such a thing could occur to a member of his family. Why on earth was she chosen for such a death when, statistically, there were so many such trips made by college students every spring?

Douglas and Danielle Ferguson shared their grief by phone. Douglas, like many parents of students at Howard Christian College, was a minister. Unlike virtually every other parent of a student at that college, however, he was a divorced minister. His marriage to Danielle lasted only a few short years after his ordination. Danielle was clearly suffocated by the life of a minister's wife. They shared custody of Cayla during her childhood years. In her teens, however, she expressed a desire to live full-time with her father, primarily because her mother lived an entirely different life: Danielle was a hard-driving corporate CEO with very little time for her daughter.

So it was Reverend Ferguson who gave the news to CEO Danielle Ferguson. For a moment or two, they were closer than they had been in twenty-two years. Yes, she said, she could be at the meeting with the State's Attorney; she would cancel a planned trip to Europe. Douglas thanked her and hung up.

Every parent of a Howard Christian College student who had been killed or injured a few weeks before was present in a large conference room in the office of the Sangamon County State's Attorney. Also present was State's Attorney Blanchard, Assistant State's Attorney Garret Nelson, Victim/Witness Coordinator Mary Walton, as well as a man who was well-known in the legal profession, Thomas Lansing. Mary and Bill Goodwin had contacted Lansing a few days earlier and had invited him to the meeting.

"Thank you for coming," Blanchard said to everyone to open the meeting. "I wanted you here, all together, first of all, to express my sympathy to all of you and to personally assure you that we intend to go after the maximum sentence for the man responsible for this terrible tragedy."

"What is that maximum sentence?" Paul Sanford asked.

"The law specifies a range of six years to 28 years," Blanchard said. "We'll be asking for the 28 years. We have no intention of plea bargaining to get a guilty plea. We feel that we will gather sufficient evidence to go to trial if necessary."

"So," said Henry Oswald, "you are absolutely certain that he'll go to prison?"

"He damn well better," Paul Sanford said. "Why don't we save the State a lot of money and just shoot the son of a bitch?"

"I understand how you feel, Mr. Sanford," the State's Attorney responded, "but, as you know, that's not how it works."

"Clearly, we're not going to shoot him," said Reverend Douglas Ferguson, although even I wouldn't pass up the opportunity if it were offered to me. The man should not ever be free to kill again."

His wife of many years ago, Danielle, assumed command. "Let's not get carried away. The fact is that the State's Attorney knows quite well what he must do. Our judicial system does not prescribe a life for a life in these cases, but we're totally in accord that the man should go to prison for as long as the law will allow.

He killed three young women and he injured another. Prison is the only place for him."

"I think we all want to do what's right," said Reverend Goodwin. That was the first contribution to the conversation by Bill Goodwin, but he had much more to say. "I am deeply saddened by the death of my daughter and your losses, but I want to see how this young man explains his behavior, and I want to see what his attitude is now. Is he remorseful? Is he uncaring of what he did? I'm not entirely sure that I want my pound of flesh before I've heard more."

Perhaps it was because of his failing voice or maybe his presence was more compelling, but everyone listened carefully to Reverend Goodwin, with one notable exception.

"I'm sorry, sir," said Paul Sanford, "but surely you are not talking forgiveness. I know that that's your business, but it's certainly not mine."

"Let me interrupt, if I may," Blanchard said. "Let's do this. Let's pursue charges against the drunk driver and prepare for trial. If he pleads guilty or is found guilty, we'll talk again before I make my final recommendation at the sentence hearing."

"Does that mean that you are now backing down from your statement that you will ask for the maximum sentence?" Paul Sanford asked.

"I have to tell you something that I'm sure you know. A crime is an offense against the State. I know you may not see it that way. You are the victims, but it is my responsibility to represent the State in pursuit of criminal charges. Certainly, I will ask for your opinion, as I said I would, but the final decision as to a recommendation to the judge will have to come from this office."

"I understand what you're saying," Danielle Ferguson interjected, "but the State hasn't suffered the deaths of our children – or the serious injury to Heather."

"John, may I?" Garret Nelson said, asking to participate in this discussion.

With a nod from Blanchard, Nelson continued. "Although a serious felony has been committed, which requires the State's action, you will also have an opportunity to bring a civil action against Walter Caine. I believe that's why Tom Lansing is here today."

Lansing had simply listened up to this point. That was all that he intended to do, but now he had been pulled into the discussion. "It's true that I'm here at the request of Reverend and Mrs. Goodwin. I will be representing them in a civil action against Caine and possibly his employer, Foster Ford."

"You intend to sue the car dealer?" Jessica Oswald asked.

"That's a possibility," Tom answered. "We're going to investigate to what extent Foster Ford might be liable under the principle of vicarious liability. We're going to explore it anyway."

"We haven't retained counsel," Henry Oswald said. "Have you?" he asked, moving his head first in Paul Sanford's direction, then, perhaps unwittingly, toward Danielle Ferguson.

Surprisingly, Douglas Ferguson responded. "No, we haven't, but I would be interested in talking to Mr. Lansing after this meeting."

"I would be very interested in having a talk with Mr. Lansing," Paul Sanford said.

"I'm not sure I'm ready to commit. We have friends who practice law in our city," Henry Oswald said, "but I would like to know what you have to say."

"If you all feel that you have time to come to my office after this meeting, I'm only a few blocks from here," Tom said.

"Do you have any more questions for me?" Blanchard asked. "If not, you should know that you can call Mary anytime with further questions. Mary, as you know, is our victim/witness coordinator. She's easier to reach than I am, but between us, we'll get your questions answered. Mary will also keep you informed about any pre-trial proceedings in case any of you want to attend."

The parents of Cayla, Maris, and Heather left John Blanchard's office with mixed feelings. On the one hand, the young State's Attorney appeared to be determined to pursue charges vigorously against the drunk driver responsible for the tragedy that involved their daughters. On the other hand, they sensed a weak link in the person of Bill Goodwin whose lust for revenge apparently did not match theirs. The man is suffering from Parkinson's, they thought. Perhaps no one would be concerned about his opinion. And how about this attorney who the Goodwins had hired? Maybe he's on to something.

Chapter Five

Tom Lansing was Springfield's best trial lawyer. Known to his colleagues at the Bar as Tom Terrific, he was prominently listed in America's Top Lawyers, a reference book published by a major law publisher. His reputation was well earned. Within a few years of his law school graduation, he was elected to the chairmanship of the Illinois State Bar Association's Young Lawyers Section. He founded his own firm after only two years as the acknowledged star of a larger firm, primarily based on his engineering three hard-fought victories for the firm. In a magnanimous gesture, he hired his brother, Mike, right out of law school and included him in the firm's name, Lansing and Lansing, as soon as Mike received word that he had passed the Bar exam and was admitted to the Bar.

It is possible that one reason for Tom Lansing's success was that he took on corporate defendants without fear. This meant contending against enormously successful trial lawyers retained by large insurance companies. Clearly, he was prepared to do that again in his representation of Patti Goodwin's parents and perhaps others involved in the same crash caused by Walter Caine.

Only two weeks before the crash, Tom Lansing had finished a case that further enhanced his reputation. Twenty-two children under ten years old had been diagnosed with a rare form of cancer over a five-year span in a small town south of Springfield. The families of these children hired Lansing and Lansing because they suspected that the cause of the cancer in their children was directly related to a chemical plant nearby. Tom hired investigators who determined that a possible source was chemicals waste dumped by the company that permeated the ground onto a children's playground. All twenty-two of the victims had spent time at that playground. Springfield lawyers marveled at the fact that Tom won a jury verdict that resulted in millions of dollars for the plaintiffs, the families of the children, and the children themselves, at least those who survived. He did all of this without proving with certainty that there was a causal relationship between the cancer and the dumping. Remarkable.

The Goodwins, the Oswalds, the Fergusons, and the Sanfords all arrived at Tom Lansing's office within a few minutes of each other after meeting in the State's Attorney's office.

"I'd like to hear more about your idea," Paul Sanford said.

"Sure," Tom replied. "I don't believe that the State's Attorney will have any difficulty getting a guilty verdict if the case goes to trial. However, I will be astonished if the drunk driver does not plead guilty. Either way, we can use that plea or that guilty verdict to prove fault in a civil action."

"Yes, I understand that, but what's this about making his employer responsible? How does that work?" Sanford asked.

"Here it is," Tom explained. "Of course, we can go after Caine and his insurance, but that would be very limited. If that were all I could do for you, I could tell you that you might not need my services. However, I'm sure that his employer, Foster Ford, has significant coverage. What we need to do is go after the employer under the principle of Respondeat Superior; that means that the employer is responsible for the acts of his employee if done in the scope of employment. Naturally, I'm talking about civil liability, not criminal liability."

Danielle Ferguson had a comment: "Surely, driving drunk can't be in the scope of employment."

"Not necessarily," Tom replied, "but we may very well have a different circumstance here. Caine was in a company car and, perhaps more importantly, the company was well aware of the practice of celebrating meeting sales quotas by partying at the end of the month."

"I don't know," Henry Oswald said. "It doesn't seem possible to me that someone can be responsible for an action of another unless that person was giving orders."

Mike Lansing, who was sitting in on the meeting, spoke for the first time. "It's called vicarious liability, the concept of being responsible for the tortuous actions of your employer or agent in certain circumstances. We handled a case last year against a company that had Christmas parties that all employees were expected to attend. Free alcohol was provided by the company. After the party, an employee ran a red light and seriously injured another driver. The company was held liable under the principle of vicarious liability."

"This is all very interesting," Paul Sanford said, "but there is no one or no way that money can make up for what's happened to my daughter and such terrible losses for the others here."

"You're absolutely right," Tom said. "Unfortunately, no civil action can make all of you whole again; all that's possible is money, so that's what we pursue."

"I really dislike asking this question," Jessica Oswald said, "but I'm assuming that the company would be liable for a great deal of money if your theory is correct. Is that right?"

"Yes, but how much would be a jury decision, unless, of course, the company's insurance company wants to settle. That is a possibility, also," Tom said. "If there is an offer from the insurance company, it will be because they decide not to risk a larger award dictated by a jury. We will let you know if there is such an offer anywhere along the line so you can participate in the decision as to whether the offer is sufficient."

Mike, the self-appointed businessman of the firm, had more to add: "Of course, our firm's percentage will be the same whether we go to trial or not, and, because we will be incurring significant expenses in preparing for trial, we also have the right to accept or turn down an offer from the insurance agency."

In civil cases, it is not unusual for a firm to turn down or accept a settlement offer, even if that rejection or acceptance frustrates or displeases its clients. Whenever a firm accepts a case, the firm puts itself in the position of a financial loss since the firm's expenses in a losing case can be quite significant. Another consideration is the time factor. In many counties, it may be as long as seven years for a case to get to trial, primarily because of crowded dockets. It could be nine or ten years in Cook County. That means that the firm is laying out money currently in hope of a damage award way down the road. The time factor adds more expenses in preserving evidence through depositions and written interrogatories. In fact, it is the time factor that often propels a settlement agreement, especially from the plaintiff side.

"Well, I don't know how the rest of you feel," Sanford said, "but I'm quite willing to have you handle the civil case for all of us if that's what everyone wants."

Ann Sanford, the Oswalds, and the Fergusons nodded.

"Just so you know, we talked to the Bar Association and researched Mr. Lansing's record before we retained him," Mary Goodwin said. "I believe that it would be to our mutual advantage to have the same legal counsel."

"If you want to discuss that without us in the room," Tom said, "we'll leave you here in the conference room as long as you want. If you agree, we can have you sign retainer forms just as the Goodwins have done already."

"There is the small matter of your fee," Danielle Ferguson said.

"I guess I'm the business of the firm," Mike Lansing said. "I want to tell you that any personal injury lawyer will charge one-third or forty per cent of the amount recovered. There are often significant expenses involved for a plaintiff's lawyer in investigations, discovery, expert witnesses. We won't charge you for any of that. We won't charge you anything unless we win. However, if all of you agree to retain our firm, our fee would be twenty-five percent of the amount received. You should feel free to check with other firms or with the Bar Association to verify what I'm telling you."

Paul Sanford once again controlled the direction of the discussion: "All of that sounds okay with me. Right now, I want to be sure that this guy gets sent away for a long, long time. What do we do to make sure that happens?"

"I think you'll find that John Blanchard and Garret Nelson will see to it that he's prosecuted to the full extent of the law," Tom said.

"I don't know about the rest of you," Sanford continued, "but I'm going to be here for every Walter Caine appearance. I want to make damn sure that this guy gets what he deserves."

Chapter Six

Three men in orange jumpsuits appeared briefly before Circuit Court Judge Byron Chase. One of them was Walter Caine. Standing beside Caine was defense attorney Norman Caswell. A few feet away, looking at a file, stood Assistant State's Attorney Garret Nelson.

"What are the charges, Mr. Nelson?" the judge asked.

Nelson read directly from the file. "The charges are four counts of Aggravated DUI resulting in a death, one count of Aggravated DUI resulting in a serious injury, and Driving Under the Influence."

Judge Chase looked at the man briefly. He knew about the crash, of course. It had appeared prominently in the newspaper for days. The arraignment would have been sooner except that Caine had to be released from the hospital and put under arrest before the arraignment could take place. "Mr. Caine," the judge said, "do you understand the charges that are being made against you today?"

"Yes, yes I do," Caine mumbled.

"How do you plead, Mr. Caine?" the judge asked.

Caine glanced at his attorney. Caswell nodded. "Not guilty, Your Honor," Walter Caine said.

"Okay," Judge Chase said, "I'm ordering a million dollar bail bond. Mr. Caine, talk to your attorney about how you might obtain your temporary release on bail."

Prosecutors have several choices on how to indict someone who has broken the law. Particularly if a death is involved, the prosecutor may opt to convene a Grand Jury to look at information presented to it to determine whether there is sufficient evidence to bring the charges. It is not the job of the Grand Jury to determine guilt or innocence, just to decide whether there is enough evidence to establish that the defendant might be guilty of the mentioned crime. There is no opportunity for a defense; the Grand Jury listens to the prosecutor's side only. It has been said by cynics that a prosecutor could get an indictment of a bologna sandwich if he or she desired to do so. A second – and more common approach – is to obtain an indictment on information directly to the judge in court. This is accomplished prior to arraignment. That process, the arraignment, is to advise the defendant exactly what charges are being brought against that defendant.

The bail amount is set by the judge. Its purpose is to insure the defendant's presence at future proceedings without the necessity of incarcerating him or her. The actual amount of cash that must be produced is only one tenth of the bail amount. Some defendants, but not many, have the cash available on their own. Some need to seek help from relatives and friends. Many need to apply to a bail bondsman who fronts the cash for a charge. Should the defendant decide to skip out of the jurisdiction, jumping bail it's called, the bail bondsman may have someone to bring the defendant back physically to protect its cash advance. Some defendants, in order to make bail, put up some collateral to secure the amount required for that one-tenth of the bail amount.

Here, the judge ordered a million dollar bail, thereby requiring Walter Caine to come up with $100,000 in order to be released from jail pending a final outcome of the case.

Norman Caswell had bail and much more to talk about when he met with Walter Caine in the county jail conference room.

"I have to tell you," Caswell said, "that the prosecution is going to have little difficulty proving its case. The lab has determined that your blood alcohol content was point 18 several hours after the crash. There is no doubt that your BAC was higher at the time of the crash. As you know, the legal limit in Illinois is point 08."

"Mr. Caswell," Caine replied, "I need to tell you something before you say anything else about a possible defense for me if any at all."

"Yes. What?"

"I want to plead guilty. I don't want to go through this sham of saying I'm not guilty or having the State prove anything. I killed three people. I'm guilty. I'm ready to accept any punishment they're going to give me."

"That's your choice, Walter," Norman said. "I wanted to give you some options based on possible approaches to my defending you, but the fact is that I think you would be doing the smart thing by pleading guilty. You know that you could face up to 28 years in prison. If you plead guilty, we might be able to work something out with the State's Attorney's office to minimize that possible sentence."

"That's not what I want, really," Walter said. "There's no need for you to do any of that. I want to accept my punishment, whatever it is."

No one simply pleads guilty to a felony when the judge asks how do you plead. Some victims and victim family members don't understand that. They are outraged to hear the defendant say in open court that he or she is not guilty. In their minds, there is no doubt that the defendant is guilty and the defendant knows he's guilty, but it's a bit more complicated than that. It is possible that someone could be not guilty even though that person committed the act that is most often, but not always, a crime. Finding a defendant not guilty or having the defendant say that he or she is not guilty doesn't mean that the defendant is not guilty, that he or she did not commit the act, because the law provides the act has to be intentional; there has to be mens rea (a phrase of interest to Latin lovers) in order for the individual to be guilty. Sometimes there is an excuse for the action that would normally be a crime – self-defense, authority to commit the act, permission given by the victim, and inability of the defendant to understand the nature of the act because of a mental impairment. Well, then, considering the last example, one might argue, why is killing someone in a drunk driving crash a crime if the defendant didn't know what he was doing when he committed the act; isn't that the same as mental illness, not understanding the act that is being performed? No, it's not, because the drunk driver purposely consumed alcoholic beverages in amounts that are known to make someone intoxicated and then a drunk driver. The mens rea exists.

"Look, Walter, I'm not certain what I can do anyway, but it's worth a try. It's my job to represent you. That means getting you found not guilty or getting you the least possible sentence. You want that, don't you?"

Walter shook his head from side to side. "I have no excuse for what I did. I expect no mercy. I just want to do what's right. I don't expect anyone to forgive me. I can't forgive myself."

"Walter, I understand what you're saying and I respect you for it, but whether you go to prison is the decision the judge will make, and he's going to make that decision based on everything he knows about you, not only that you were intoxicated and were responsible for a tragedy. That's how the system works."

"What else is there that means anything?" Walter asked.

"Your life, your whole life. You have never had a DUI, you've never broken the law, and you are a responsible, hard-working family man with a wife and a four-year-old son."

"That's not entirely true," Caine said.

"What do you mean?" Norman asked.

Caine spoke haltingly: "Debby – my wife – and I haven't been getting … along. We were heading for a divorce. Of course, that's certainly going to happen now."

"Have you talked to her since you've been in the county jail?"

Walter sat slumped forward unable to look Norman in the eye. "No … and that really worries me. Johnny's only four years old. I know that she's going to try to take him away from me. I guess that's all for the best now."

Norman sat back and spoke softly: "So celebrating quotas was not the only reason for drinking that night."

"No. No, it wasn't," Walter said. "I was down, all right, all day. I tried to hide it the best I could. I hadn't told anyone, didn't want to spoil the fun, I guess."

"Walter, I'm going to ask you a very important question. Please be honest with me. You know that I can't reveal anything you tell me because of lawyer-client privilege."

"You want to know if I got on the exit intentionally."

"Yes," Norman said. "Did you?"

"I don't know. I had way too much to drink, and I was all confused about what was happening to my marriage. I don't remember what I was thinking. I hope to God that I didn't get on the highway purposely to kill myself only to kill those girls. What I did was terrible enough."

"If it makes you feel any better," Norman said, "with at least a point 18 BAC, I doubt that you were thinking about much of anything at all."

"Nothing is going to make me feel any better. My life is over no matter why I drank so much."

"Let's get you out of the jail cell, Walter," Norman said. "I think that I can get your bail reduced to $500,000. That's $50,000 in cash. No one expects that you'll leave town. Will you?"

"No, I'm not going anywhere. My parents have come to see me. They want me to live with them until … well, until I'm sentenced to prison."

"Can you raise $50,000? That's what you'll need to do, raise some of the bail money? You own your home, I understand. Also, I believe that your parents want to help if you need them to do that."

"I should be able to raise the money," Caine said. "I've already put an awful burden on my parents in so many ways."

"Okay, I'll make the bail reduction motion. We'll talk again soon. Let's hold off on that guilty plea for the time being."

Chapter Seven

As promised, Paul Sanford was in attendance at the status hearing. The other parents of the crash victims opted not to attend a proceeding that surely would take no more than three minutes. Judges don't like to have felony charges unresolved on their calendars for extended periods. Consequently, sometimes monthly, they have the prosecutors and defense attorneys appear in court either to state that they are ready to go to trial or that they need more time, for the usual reasons – further investigation required, more discovery needed, the defendant not physically or mentally able to participate in his or her defense.

Walter Caine's participation in the process was minimal. He stood next to his attorney, Norman Caswell, when his case was called. Caswell asked for a postponement without stating a reason. The judge might allow that in the early going, and the prosecution had no objection. The Sixth Amendment of the United States Constitution does require a "speedy trial" in criminal cases, intended to ensure that defendants are not subjected to an unreasonably lengthy incarceration prior to a fair trial, but the right is typically defined by state statutes and doesn't really kick in unless the State has failed to bring a case to trial for a prolonged period. If that occurs, that may be a cause for dismissal of a criminal charge. However, statutes typically include exemption to the speedy trial rule such as a delay due to the request of the defense or if the prosecution has good cause for the delay.

"This case will be put on the docket for status clarification next month," the judge said, looking at his calendar. "The fourteenth."

Counsel on both sides nodded. Caine had nothing to say or do except stand there in front of the judge during the aforementioned three minutes. He then turned, with his attorney, and walked toward the courtroom exit. In the meantime, Paul Sanford left his seat in the courtroom and walked out before Caine and Caswell reached the exit. Sanford was waiting for them just outside of the courtroom. He took a step toward Caine and pointed a finger at him.

"I hope you die a terrible death and go directly to hell, you son of a bitch," Sanford screamed at him. As he said this, he took a menacing step toward Walter.

Both the elderly bailiff, who was standing near the exit of the courtroom, and Norman Caswell instinctively put an arm between Caine and Paul Sanford.

"Sir," the bailiff said, "you're going to have to get hold of yourself."

Norman immediately grabbed Walter by the arm and took him into a nearby conference room.

"You're not going to get away with what you've done," Sanford hollered after him.

"You're going to have to leave, sir," the guard said. 'If you are disruptive in the future, the judge won't allow you in the courtroom."

"I'm sorry, I'm sorry," Walter mumbled as Norman led him into the conference room and away from a very angry Paul Sanford.

It was difficult to determine whether Sanford's anger was genuine or simple grandstanding. Certainly, he had no intention of attacking Walter Caine. Strangely, he abided by the rules in the courtroom itself but then exercised his belligerence immediately outside of the room in the corridor. If, indeed, he had been similarly disruptive inside of the courtroom, in the judge's presence, he could have found himself arrested and in the county jail for contempt of court.

While this was occurring in Springfield, Illinois, Baptist minister Douglas Ferguson and CEO Danielle Ferguson were having lunch in a Trenton, New Jersey, restaurant. Although they had long divorced, having lunch together was not extraordinary. The lunches began as a monthly exchange of views on matters affecting Cayla. Although no one would consider them friends, the Cayla link was all that was required for them to maintain a relationship that appeared to work for both of them. Many financial decisions concerning Cayla's education were made in this way, mostly cooperatively. Now that Cayla was gone, the lunches continued to deal with the many issues emanating from Cayla's death.

"I don't know when it's going to get easier," the Reverend Douglas Ferguson said. "Somehow, I keep forgetting she's gone. The phone rings and immediately I think it's her calling from school."

"I know it's a very large adjustment in your life," Danielle Ferguson said. "After all, she lived with you until she left for college. Sure, we had some weekends together, and we shared a few weeks vacation each year, but that didn't make me a good mother, I know. I always thought that I'd make it up to her some day, somehow."

"You know," Reverend Ferguson said, "I was thinking the other night that we never really said goodbye. When she went out with her friends, it was See you later or Peace, Dad, or Ta ta – never goodbye. Even when she left for school, it was simply: Take care, Dad. Now it's too late to say goodbye."

Danielle held back uncharacteristic tears. "I'm not sure I want to go to Springfield any more. I know I should be there for Cayla, but there's so much sorrow, so much anger."

"It's odd," Douglas replied. "Three fathers and three mothers lost their daughters. We're all sad and angry, but this man Sanford is angriest of all, and his child survived. She's probably going to be all right."

"I think part of that is a form of survivor guilt. It's pretty common. Someone survives when others die. Survivors can't understand why they didn't die, so they feel guilty about it. That's been extended, I think, to Heather's father. She survived; he feels guilty, so he's overcompensating by demonstrating it with rage, proving that he's angrier about what happened than all of the rest of us."

"Danielle, maybe you'd better get back to your profit and loss statements and European trips. Leave the psychology to the psychologists. Anyway, my whole point is that all of this anger is expected of us, but is it really necessary? The man was drunk; he didn't intentionally cause deaths. No matter how we look at it, it was an accident."

"Intentional or not, the law says he has to go to prison," Danielle said. "I just want to get it all over with. We have prosecutors and a trial lawyer telling us what we should and shouldn't be doing or feeling. I'd like to put all this legal maneuvering behind us. Then, we can just try to remember how Cayla lived, not how she died. We can concentrate on the good times. She was personable, attractive, and smart, smarter in many ways than either of us. Anyway, I'll be in London for a few weeks. After that, I'll be wherever my company needs me until … well, until I go to Springfield for the sentencing of the man who took our Cayla's life."

"God help us all," the minister said.

Chapter Eight

It's not unusual for a defense attorney to request a meeting with the prosecution. Norman Caswell's reputation was not built on getting defendants off. He was known and respected because he did all he could for his client. Sometimes, the best advice is to have the client admit guilt. Then, his goal was to minimize the client's punishment. That's why he made an appointment to see State's Attorney Blanchard and Assistant State's Attorney Nelson.

"We'll listen to what you have to say, Norm," said Blanchard, "but I've made my policy on plea negotiating very clear."

"John, I'm here to ask for very little," Norman said. "What I'm going to suggest will simplify the whole process, make your job a whole lot easier, and cause considerably less apprehension for the victims' families."

"Okay, I'm listening," the State's Attorney said.

"My guy will plead guilty to the most serious charge – Aggravated DUI resulting in multiple deaths. That will subject him to a possible 28-year sentence. All other charges get dropped. That's not a deal, John; it's common sense."

Blanchard turned to Nelson. "What do you think, Garret?"

"You make a good argument, Norm, especially concerning the families of the victims and the victim who survived and her parents." He turned toward Blanchard. "This would not be a bit unusual, John."

"The problem is that I've promised the parents right here in this office that I would prosecute to the extent of the law," Blanchard responded.

"It's your decision, John," Nelson said. "You know that, but I agree with Norm that keeping the most serious charge and getting a guilty plea is not really plea negotiating. As long as we are not reducing the charges or the possible sentence, I think we're fine. Anyway, we know that if he were to be found guilty at trial on all charges, he would serve sentences concurrently."

There are some sentences that can be served consecutively, when there are markedly different crimes, even though they emanate from the same occurrence. However, several counts of the same crime with additional charges that are contained in the more serious charge result, by statute, in concurrent sentences. Consequently, the defendant serves the time ordered in the longer sentence.

"Okay, Norm, we've got a deal. ...No, not a deal, an arrangement that will result in a guilty plea and a satisfactory resolution of the case."

Walter Caine was in Norman Caswell's office when he heard the news.

"We're on the docket for the fourteenth, as you know. We'll be using that date for the guilty plea. The State's Attorney has agreed to drop all charges except for the one, unfortunately, that can send you to prison for a long time."

"I think that's best," Walter said. "I'm ready to plead guilty and accept whatever sentence is given me."

"Look, Walter, I have one more idea that I'd like to put into play if you'll let me."

Walter shrugged. "I don't know. What do you have in mind?"

Norman thought for a moment. He wanted to express his suggestion in a way that would be amenable to his client. "I know you have genuine remorse for what happened. That's clear. I'd like to suggest that you volunteer to spend some time speaking to college and high school students about what you did. You might be able to make a major contribution to preventing DUI deaths in the future."

"There's no question that I would do that if anyone thought it would help," Walter said, "but that could be a long way off."

"I know that, Walter. It's highly unlikely, of course, that the judge will consider a short prison term, but if he does, this offer could influence his decision on the period of imprisonment."

"If the judge thought that my speaking would genuinely help, I would really want to do that, but I don't think it should have any impact on my sentence."

"It's a remote possibility that the judge would give the idea much consideration anyway," Norman said, "but I do want to get it in at the sentencing hearing."

"Do you think that the judge will look at this as a genuine offer and not…"

"Playing him? No, I've appeared before this judge a fair number of times. I think he would believe you're sincere if in fact you are sincere. Would you want to do this if there was an opportunity to do so even if it's twenty-some years down the road? If we had a slight chance for probation, I think that this proposal would be much more effective."

"Of course, I don't know how I'll feel after a long term in prison," Walter said, "but I would really want to do that if there were any chance that it would help prevent the kind of terrible thing that I've caused. It just seems to me that high school kids would wonder why I'm there instead of in prison. I would want to help if they would let me; I just don't know how much it would help."

Norman thought about this response for a few seconds. "Walter, I made the suggestion as a method of mitigating your sentence. You've turned it around on me. I think the judge will determine this to be a genuine offer because you've convinced me that you're genuine."

Norman wasn't easily moved by one of his clients. It was usually the case that his clients were undoubtedly guilty of the crime being charged. In such a case, he had to deal with the fact that he was providing a defense for a guilty man. Consequently, he demanded the truth from his client, not lies and lame excuses. This client, however, told the truth but, surprisingly, did not look for a way out of being convicted and punished. Since there was no doubt of Caine's guilt, Norman would lock onto Caine's remorse as his best and probably only line of defense.

The Goodwins were in the courtroom when Walter Caine pleaded guilty. So were the Oswalds, Douglas Ferguson, and, of course, Paul Sanford with his wife, Ann. Victim Witness/Coordinator Mary Walton had called the families to inform them of the expected plea. Since the courtroom was crowded with a few friends of the families, readers of the local newspaper who had developed an interest in the case, and representatives of the press and television stations throughout central Illinois, it may not have been apparent to anyone except Paul Sanford that a Sheriff's Deputy was seated directly behind him.

Judge Byron Chase called the case, and Walter Caine and his attorney once again stood before the Bench. This time, he did participate.

"I understand, Mr. Caine, that you are here to change your plea to the charge of Aggravated DUI resulting in multiple deaths and that all other charges against you have been dismissed."

Although the families had been notified of the guilty plea, the State's Attorney's office did not relate the additional information that other charges had been dismissed. The judge's statement elicited no reaction from the crash parents save for one. Sanford flushed. His immediate thought was that Walter Caine would not be punished for Heather's injury. He seethed.

Walter Caine replied with a nod from Norman Caswell. "Yes, Your Honor, I now want to plead guilty to that charge."

"By pleading guilty, you are waiving all rights to a trial that you are entitled to under the U.S. Constitution. Are you pleading guilty with full knowledge that you are waiving those rights?"

"Yes, I am, Your Honor," Caine replied.

"Is it correct that you have been made no promises by the prosecution or any others that a guilty plea will entitle you to any special treatment?"

"Yes, Your Honor," Caine said. "I'm pleading guilty because I'm guilty. I was totally responsible for the terrible thing that I did."

"Mr. Caine, I am advising you that you have a right to withdraw your plea up until your sentencing for this crime but cannot withdraw the plea after that time unless there is a valid, legal reason for doing so. Do you understand that?"

"Yes."

"All right," Judge Chase said. "I'm going to accept your plea of guilty." The judge looked toward Garret Nelson and Norman Caswell. "I am ordering a pre-sentence investigation and will put the sentencing hearing on the calendar for ... September 30."

As Caine turned to leave the courtroom, the tears that ran down his face glistened from the overhead lights. This image was observed and not forgotten by Reverend Bill Goodwin.

As promised in Mary Walton's phone calls to the crash victims' parents, John Blanchard met with all of them save for Danielle Ferguson who did not attend the guilty plea. Blanchard wanted the meeting primarily to address optional participation by the parents in the sentencing hearing. Paul Sanford wasn't ready for that discussion quite yet.

"What happened to the charges based on the injuries to my daughter?" Sanford asked.

"I wish that the law allowed consecutive sentences," Blanchard said. "Then, we would be looking at penalties for each charge. That would put him away most likely for life. Unfortunately, that's not how it works. When there are victims from a single occurrence, as here, and there are multiple charges, even if the defendant is convicted on all charges, the court would hand down sentences that would be served concurrently."

"So, it's impossible to get a greater sentence than the one provided by the most severe charge," added Garret Nelson.

"But why drop the other charges?" Sanford asked. "If he says he's guilty of killing three young women in that crash, he's certainly guilty of injuring my daughter."

"If we pursued that charge and had to go to trial, all of you would have had to accept trial delays because of defense motions and then a trial that would have been painful for all of you because it would have required reliving that night through testimony of police officers, the emergency medical team, the hospital personnel. We had an offer to have him plead guilty to a charge that's going to send him to prison for a long time. We are going to recommend the maximum sentence, 28 years."

"All right," Sanford said. "I still don't like it very much, but I understand what you're doing, and I realize it's your decision. I just hope that this move results in the 28 years."

"Let's talk about the sentencing hearing," Blanchard said. "The judge has ordered a pre-sentence report. That means that the Probation Department will investigate and report on Caine's life essentially, especially any criminal record. The judge will know if he ever committed a crime or even had a traffic violation. If it's determined that he has any negative record, the judge will take that into consideration in determining the sentence."

"What else will he consider?" Reverend Ferguson asked.

"We have an opportunity to convince the judge that a severe sentence should be handed down," Blanchard answered. "The defense will have an opportunity to convince the judge that the sentence should not be so long as we would like. They'll do that by having individuals testify that he's remorseful, that his life has changed, whatever."

"Does all of that really make a difference?" Jessica Oswald asked.

"Let me tell you," Garret Nelson said, "that I've been through this many times. They could put a mother, a wife, a minister on the stand. As far as I can tell, it makes very little if any difference in the judge's decision, so don't let anything you hear upset you if it's coming from anyone testifying in mitigation for the defendant."

"What does make a difference, I think," said Blanchard, "are the victim impact statements. It is your right to read a statement to the judge that lets the judge know how the loss of your daughters impacted your lives. Mary will give you a set of questions that will help you prepare your statements. She'll need to have these at least a week before the hearing."

"What if we don't want to give this …this victim impact statement?" Mary Goodwin asked.

Mary Walton, the perfectly quiet and unobtrusive victim/witness coordinator, thought that she could help. "I'll be happy to help you in any way that I can. If you don't want to read your statement in court, you can just give it to me and we'll see to it that the judge gets it. We need to give him all of the statements anyway before the hearing, whether you're going to read them in court or not. If you wish, you can prepare a joint statement from each family. Of course, if you don't want to prepare a statement, that's up to you."

"Let me get something straight," Paul Sanford said. "We all agree that we want the maximum sentence for this guy, right?"

"I think, Mr. Sanford," Reverend Ferguson said, "that each of us should make our own feelings known to the judge. I think that he'll make his own decision, anyway. Frankly, I doubt that our victim impact statement will make much difference."

"They might, Reverend Ferguson," Nelson said. "In any case, this is your opportunity to express your strong feelings to the judge before he decides on the sentence."

"Please work with Mary on completing your statements and getting them to me," the State's Attorney said. "Also, let Mary know if you want to read your statement at the hearing. For my part, I intend to ask for the maximum sentence of 28 years."

Chapter Nine

Heather's recovery progressed well, although there was lingering pain, she still needed crutches, and a cast would remain on her forearm for a few more weeks after the scheduled sentencing date. Her father encouraged her to make the trip to Springfield. He also was certain that his daughter's presence would go a long way toward convincing the judge that a long sentence was appropriate.

What Paul Sanford didn't realize was that Heather had conflicted feelings about many of the issues emanating from the crash. While her father's stance appeared to be a simple form of revenge, Heather's physical and mental well being was based on much more than that. She had to have a frank and open discussion of these concerns with her parents. Now, however, she didn't have to deal with her parents all by herself. Both of her older sisters, Elaine and Carrie, were there for moral support.

"I'm not sure I want to go to the sentencing," Heather said.

"I'd like to have the judge see what that bastard did to you," her father replied. "You don't have to speak. Just sit in the courtroom with us."

"I don't know," Heather said.

"You've been uncharacteristically quiet about all of this, Elaine," Ann said. "After all, you're the lawyer in the family."

"Mom, I do searches for a title company. I know virtually nothing about criminal law," Elaine responded, "but if she doesn't want to go, we shouldn't make her go."

"Daddy," joined in Carrie, "for God's sake, she's still hurting. Let the parents who lost their daughters handle this."

The ever impatient Paul Sanford snapped at his two older daughters. "Don't you two want to see this guy get punished for what he did? Just look at your sister. Think about her friends who were murdered."

"Dad," Elaine said. "It wasn't murder. You know that. It was a terrible accident caused by a man who was drunk."

"That's enough," Sanford replied.

"What do we know about this man," Carrie asked, "except that he was inebriated and drove on the wrong side of the highway? Do we know anything about him personally?"

"I know quite a bit about him," Ann said. "Mary Walton from the State's Attorney's office told me about him."

"Who he is, is not relevant," Sanford said.

"Can we hear it anyway, Mom?" Elaine asked.

"Whatever," Sanford snapped.

"He's married but possibly in the middle of a divorce," Ann explained. "He has a four-year-old son, he's the finance manager at that car dealer's, and he's 28 years old."

"Has he been arrested for drunk driving in the past?" Carrie asked.

"She didn't know about that," Ann said, "but their Probation Department is looking into it before the sentencing. If he has, the judge will take that into consideration."

"Since he was drunk this time," Sanford said, "I bet he's driven drunk before. Maybe he just hasn't been caught."

"We don't know that, Paul," Ann said. "And obviously, he's very upset himself. You saw him cry when he pleaded guilty, I know you did."

"Yeah, he was crying," Sanford replied. "He was crying because he knows he's going to prison. That's what the tears are about. You're going to see him cry again at the hearing. You can bet on that. He's probably been practicing that act."

"We're discussing this as though we were the victims," Elaine said. "I think we should know how Heather feels. Look at all she's been through."

"I'm not sure how I feel," Heather said. "I think that this man has to be punished. He killed three people. I think it's up to those parents and the judge to decide."

"All right, don't go," Sanford said. "I'm going to let you four bleeding hearts do nothing. I'm going to be there, and I'm going to make sure that the other parents are supported when they give their statements."

Paul Sanford stepped out of the room, having no more patience for his wife and daughters.

"I think Dad should just cool it," Elaine said. "He's not going to accomplish anything by showing how angry he is."

"You're talking about your father, Elaine," Ann said. "That's all he knows."

"You know," Elaine said, addressing Heather, "forget the drunk driver. What's important is getting you back. Is there anything we can do?"

"The doctor says that the bones are mending," Heather said, "and I'll be able to walk without these crutches in a month or so. This arm cast is going to be with me for a while, but, as you know, I'm right-handed, so I'll be able to take notes, I guess."

"Wait a minute," Carrie said. "You're not thinking of going back to school when the semester starts."

"Are you, Heather?" Ann asked, obviously surprised at the idea.

"I've been on the phone with my advisor. She says they can help me catch up."

"Your father's not going to like that idea," Ann said. "He doesn't want you going back to that school at all, certainly not now."

Heather had already decided. "I can't stay here and wrap myself in a big security blanket of self-pity. I'm going back to school."

"Are you sure you're thinking straight about this?" asked Elaine.

"That's the most relevant question I've been asked," Heather said. "Is my brain still functioning right? Anyway, I need a mocha. Anybody for Starbucks?"

"I'll go with," Carrie said.

It was at Starbucks that Heather revealed some astonishing information.

"My brain is taking me to strange places," Heather told Carrie. "Right after the crash, while I was in the hospital, I couldn't remember what I was told ten minutes before."

"My God, Heather," exclaimed Carrie. "Are you still having the problem? You can't go to school like that. It would be dangerous."

"No, that's not it, Carrie. There's something stranger going on. Some freakish thing has happened to my memory."

"Freakish?" Carrie asked. "What do you mean? Are you having trouble remembering what just happened or what happened long ago or is it your studies that you can't remember?"

"Oddly, not any of that … I'm remembering things from long ago, events that may or may not have happened."

"Wow!" Carrie was intrigued.

"I don't know if I should tell you this, but, for the first time, I'm having a very bad memory," Heather said.

Carrie hated to ask because it was clear that Heather was very uncomfortable with what she sorely wanted to tell her sister. Nevertheless, she had no choice. "What's it all about, Heather?"

"It's about Dad. Now, I feel that it was always there, but, since the accident, this thing has somehow emerged."

"Are you saying that Dad did something wrong?"

"God, this is awful," Heather said, "but I remember Dad touching me … as he shouldn't have … when I was maybe five or six. Carrie, I wouldn't tell this to just anyone, but that's what I'm remembering."

"No, Heather, it couldn't be. Something bizarre has happened to your memory. That has to be the answer."

"I wish that I could believe that, but the image is so clear. What should I do?"

Repression involves placing uncomfortable thoughts in primarily inaccessible areas of the mind. When something occurs that can't be dealt with in the present, it might be pushed away, with a subconscious effort to deal with it at another time or to have it merely fade away. It is possible, then, that Heather experienced trauma when she was only five and then again a distinctively different trauma fifteen years later? The brain is a mysterious, complex organ. Would vastly different forms of trauma somehow ignite memories that the brain wants to displace and yet retain?

There were no qualms about attending the sentencing hearing in the home of Henry and Jessica Oswald. They gathered their four surviving daughters in the living room. The girls ranged in age from a six-year-old to a teenager to the two daughters who were older than Maris at 22 and 24.

With Henry's penchant for numbers and analysis, he knew precisely what he was going to do with his life and now with his victim impact statement and his attendance at the hearing. Jessica also was an extremely organized person. While she thoroughly enjoyed her daughters, much of her time was devoted to the multiple flower gardens surrounding the Oswald home. Henry had done well as a Certified Public Accountant. Very early in his career, he founded his own firm, one that became very successful in a short time. This intense, exact work ethic that was demonstrated by both Henry and Jessica not surprisingly resulted in a decision that they would be present at the hearing and that they would do their utmost to convince the judge that Walter Caine should go to prison for many, many years.

"As you know, everyone, your mother and I will be in Illinois for a few days," Henry began. "This will be the end of the criminal process against the man who took your sister's life. I believe that the judge will send him to prison. We want to be there for Maris. We're still involved in a civil suit because of that crash, but getting the criminal matter out of the way will allow us to turn more of our attention to honoring Maris in some other ways that we have in mind."

"Do you think the judge will sentence him to the 28-year prison term?" asked his oldest daughter, Mary.

Ever the CPA, Henry responded with numbers. "If they do, he may be released sooner than the full sentence period. The law says that no matter how well he behaves in prison, he still must serve 85 per cent of the time. In other words, if it's 28 years, he would have to serve, let me see, that would be almost 24 years. And if the sentence is 24 years, say, he would have to serve about 20 and a half years."

"How do you do that in your head?" asked his youngest daughter, Madeline.

"Oh, that's just my business, Honey," Henry responded.

"Anyway," Jessica added, "I know that you will get along fine without us for this short time. Of course, we'll have our cell phones with us if you need us. I think that we have to honor Maris by living exceptional lives. I'll always be proud of what Maris did with her life. I loved having five daughters. Now, the four of you will always make me proud, I'm sure."

Chapter Ten

The mood was certainly grim when Walter Caine met once again with his attorney, Norman Caswell. Also present were Mr. and Mrs. Edward Caine, Walter's parents. This was the last meeting of the group before the sentencing hearing. All issues of payment to Caswell had been resolved. Much to Norman's relief, he did not have to bill Ed and Betty Caine for services provided to their son. Walter had been industrious. His home mortgage had been paid off in a remarkable five years through accelerated payments. It was in his name only since he purchased it before his marriage. He was fortunate that the house sold at a premium price a few weeks after it was on the market. He paid off the bail lien, which would be returned to him by the county in any case since he did not bolt, and he had funds to pay his legal fees, possible criminal fines, and money to help pay a civil judgment against him, although he had no idea how much he would be liable for in a civil suit. Of course, he had insurance, but he certainly did not have the kind of coverage that would pay for damage awards for three deaths and a serious injury.

"As you know," Norman said, "we have an opportunity to persuade the judge to give you a sentence that is less than the 28-year maximum provided by the law. I hope that either or both of you, Ed and Betty, will testify as to Walter's character and that you can help me get a few other people to testify."

"I know that we're willing to speak for our son," Ed Caine said, "but I think that Betty could do a better job. She's more … what's the word … articulate."

"Betty, what do you think? Can you do that?" Norman asked.

"Yes, I could. How would that work? Will you be asking me some questions?"

"Yes, and I'll go over them with you before you leave today," Norman answered. And I think that it might be best if only one of you testified. We don't want to overdo, but we would like to have you let the judge know what Walter is really like."

"Our son has always been a hard worker, a good father, and, overall, a good man. This should never have happened," Betty Caine said.

"That's what we're going to get at with my questions. Now, you should know that the prosecutor will be able to ask you questions also. He may or may not. Just answer whatever questions he asks."

"Mr. Caswell," Walter said, "I appreciate what you're trying to do, but I don't feel right doing it. You know how I feel. If it's meant for me to go to prison for a long time for what I did, I don't think we should try to prevent that. I deserve it."

"Walter," Norman said, "you deserve what the judge believes you deserve when he has all the facts. We need to make sure he knows who you are. That's one of the facts."

"Whatever you say, Mr. Caswell. I just can't help how I feel."

Norman continued his attempt to get information that would help. "I know, but let's see what happens. Have you been going to church since the crash and did you go before that time?"

"I have always gone to church. I was raised as a Catholic. My family always went to church, and I went with them. I could never get my wife to go. She said she didn't believe in organized religion. But I always took Johnny with me."

"Good," Norman said, "and do you know the priest personally at your church?"

"Father Higgins will surely help us," Betty said.

"Good, good. Now, how about friends or neighbors?"

"I don't suppose I can ask any of my co-workers," Walter said. "I haven't heard from any of them."

"No, I think we'll pass on co-workers," Norman said. "Lansing may be calling some of them in the civil action."

Norman turned toward Betty: "Did Walter give you much trouble when he was a kid?"

"Truly, he was always the perfect child. I can't think of anything that Walter did that ever was a problem for us."

"Surely you were unhappy with something, sometime."

"He knows," Betty answered, "that we thought he made a bad decision when he married Debby. He knew her for only a few months, but when Johnny came along, we were thrilled that he did get married."

"What do you know about his drinking habits?" Norman asked.

"We never knew that he was much of a drinker. I think he was just trying to be sociable that night and wasn't accustomed to drinking that much."

"Tell me about his behavior since the crash," Norman said. "What can you tell me about that?"

Betty shook her head slowly from side to side. "He's been very helpful to us around the house, and he took a part-time job with my brother who runs a hardware store, but that's just temporary until we see what happens."

"What's has his mood been like since the accident?"

"He's been sad. I know that he thinks about it a lot, but we don't talk about it much."

"As for as you know, Betty, has Walter been drinking?"

"No, I'm sure that he's not drinking," Betty said.

"Okay, Betty. I'm just going to ask you some questions like those. We'll have just a few of you testifying as to Walter's character and about his feelings about the accident. Let's stick with friends outside of work, Father Higgins, and you, Betty," Norman concluded.

How about those co-workers? Paul, who had helped Walter into the car in Friday's parking lot that night, met with Foster Ford's CEO, Harry Foster, shortly after the crash. At the time of their conversation, Harry needed much more information about the crash. While he felt great sympathy for the victims, his first instinct, of course selfishly, was to save his business. Consequently, he had issued an order to all employees not to talk to the press or anyone else without his permission. The anyone else included investigators from the State's Attorney's office and plaintiff law firms.

"I take it," Harry said to Paul, "that all of you drank too much that night. Isn't that right?"

"Harry," Paul responded, "I don't know more about this terrible thing than anybody else. Yes, we were all drinking, but I guess some people can hold their liquor better than some others."

"I'm talking to you first, Paul, for obvious reasons. You and Walter were great buddies. Everybody knows that."

Paul exhaled deeply. "Sure, we're friends. I even offered to drive him to the party."

"Why didn't he take your offer?" Harry asked.

"It was a no-brainer. He had a company car and he could go straight home whenever he wanted."

"Did you see him leave?" Harry asked.

"I don't remember," Paul lied. "I don't know when he left. I'm not a brother's keeper kind of guy."

"Don't give me that bull," Harry shouted. "There's no way that he would have left without your knowing it."

"All right, I helped him out. I asked him if he could drive. Sure, he said. How could I know he was too high to drive? I was four sheets to the wind myself."

"Look, I don't think any of us can be charged with a crime," Harry said, "unless they charge us with perjury or something. Walter was the drunk driver. He's the only one who committed a crime."

"They're going to be here to question us, aren't they?" Paul asked.

"Yes, and we're going to have to tell the truth, especially to the State's Attorney's guys," Harry said. "We're going to get everybody who was at that party together this afternoon and get our stories straight before those bastards descend on us."

Have you ever watched a car dealer doing a pitch on television? There is probably no stunt, sometimes even involving animals, that is beneath the hustle level of these guys. Harry was masterful at these ridiculous commercials. It didn't matter what he did in front of a camera as long as he and his car dealership were remembered. The real razzle-dazzle, of course, came when the customer walked onto the lot.

Harry built his car dealership on promotion, promotion, and promotion along with training his sales staff to close the deal. Now, he had forebodings of losing it all. That's why he called his insurance company and was immediately hooked up with the firm of Collins, Gunther, Price, and Dean and, more specifically, senior partner Malcolm Collins. National Security Insurance had the firm on retainer and had the unfortunate reputation of fighting insurance claims that amounted to more than $100,000 or so. When Harry's personal phone rang, he saw Collins et al on caller I.D.

"This is Harry Foster," was his phone pick-up announcement.

"Mr. Foster, this is Malcolm Collins. I understand you're expecting my call."

Chapter Eleven

Judge Byron Chase looked out toward a packed courtroom. Maybe he should have switched courtrooms for this hearing, he thought. But, then, that wasn't his problem. It simply means that some people would have to stand in the back of the room. As usual, the media was there; after all, this case was discussed in the papers, on radio, and on television for the past few months. He knew that family members of victims were there and that he would be hearing from some of them. Their victim impact statements were already part of his file, and he had read them, but only one demanded more attention than the others. That one he had read more carefully.

There were also many friends of the victims in attendance. In fact, a bus carrying students had arrived early that morning from Howard Christian College. Added to that group were members of the community who wanted to participate in a happening event. Oh, yes, Walter Caine had some supporters, also, old friends and family members, both near and distant. All of the parents of the young women killed in the crash were present including the busy Danielle Ferguson. Obvious to them, however, was the absence of the Heather Sanford family, especially Paul Sanford.

As expected, Norman Caswell put Father Higgins on the stand first. He testified that he had met with Walter on several occasions after Walter attended Sunday Mass since the crash took place. Walter was truly remorseful, he said, and it would be a terrible waste to put a young man behind bars for a dreadful, tragic mistake when he could be serving the community instead. In answer to Norman's questions, he speculated that if Walter had a chance to perform some good in the community, that would be a better sentence.

"Do you believe that Walter Caine has changed since the accident?" Norman asked the priest.

"I believe he is the same good man he was before the accident," Father Higgins said, "except that now he is steeped in guilt and depression because of that terrible event."

Norman Caswell had carefully coached everyone who was to testify in Walter's behalf to use the word accident instead of the word crash. It was semantics, of course, but accident had a less damning connotation, moving minds more toward a faultless action. Of course, this crash was not an accident in anyone's judgment.

A life-long friend, Jerry Haas, testified next. He confirmed that Walter was always well-liked and well behaved.

"He wouldn't hurt a fly," was Jerry's estimation of the defendant.

"Have you known Walter Caine to be a law abiding, good citizen?" Norman asked.

"Law abiding and God-fearing," Haas answered.

The only surprise in Mr. Haas' testimony was when he admitted, upon cross-examination by Garret Nelson, that Walter Caine tended to have "a heavy foot."

Betty Caine took the stand and testified that Walter was her only son and that he had always been good to his parents.

"Is he still helpful to you and your husband?" asked Norman.

"Very much so," Betty said. "My husband, Ed, has been suffering from back problems for years. He's unable to do much work around the house. Walter comes over often to mow the lawn, put out the garbage, fix anything that's been broken - that kind of thing."

"So you would find it difficult not to have this ongoing help?" Norman asked.

This was clearly a leading question, but neither Blanchard nor Nelson thought that it was worthwhile to object. They let it ride.

"Yes, I just don't know what we'll do without his help."

That would be it in an effort to win a lesser sanction for Walter, save for Norman's argument to the judge just prior to a decision.

John Blanchard's job was not to prove guilt; Walter had pleaded guilty. He presented testimony in aggravation, that is, he wanted to demonstrate that a stiffer sentence was necessary because of the extreme acts of the defendant in committing the crime. He put Illinois State Police Sergeant Kirk Olden on the stand, the first man to arrive at the scene of the crash.

After establishing Sergeant Olden's twenty years of service as a State Policeman, John Blanchard began the questioning: "Sergeant, please tell us what you saw when you arrived at the scene of the crash on Routes 55 and 72 during the early morning hours of April 30, 2001."

"Yes, sir. I saw two vehicles off one side of the highway. They were totally torn apart, especially the students' car, with pieces of steel and contents scattered along the road. There were also several limbs that had been torn from the victims as a result of the crash. The grass along the side of the road was sprayed with blood. It was the worst crash I've ever seen."

"What action did you take at that time?" Norman asked.

"I knew that other officers were on the way to the scene. I verified by phone that EMTs were on the way. We needed to get the victims to emergency care, although it appeared that three of the women had died on impact from what we could tell. We placed warning lights on the highway and rerouted traffic to avoid any further accidents."

"Did you see Walter Caine behind the wheel of the other vehicle?" Norman asked.

"Yes, I did."

"Can you describe this vehicle?"

"Yes, it was a black Ford Taurus with dealer plates."

"Please describe Walter Caine's demeanor and relate any words that he may have said when you first saw him."

The State Policeman shook his head slowly. "He was frantic. He was pinned in the vehicle, shouting at me."

"What was he saying?" Norman asked.

"My God, what have I done, what have I done?"

"What happened then?"

"He was removed from the vehicle and taken to emergency. His blood was drawn both by the hospital for determining necessary treatment and by a police officer who determined that a blood draw could and should be taken."

"Do you know what the result of the draw was, Sergeant?"

"Yes, he had a point one eight BAC."

And you said that was the worst crash you had ever seen in twenty years of service as a police officer?"

"Yes, I still can't get the image out of my mind," Sergeant Olden said. "That night, after I completed all the paper work, I have to admit that I went home and just cried. Those poor women."

Policemen, too, are human beings, after all. Although they are trained to deal with violence and tragedies, they are not above being affected by what they see and hear. While they may develop a hard exterior and are expected to be calm and unemotional in dealing with situations, anyone who knows a police officer personally knows that they can be personable, friendly, and caring, just like anyone else.

As he relived what he saw, big, tough, hardened Sergeant Olden fought back more tears.

It had been determined by the parents that a joint statement would be read for each of the parents. Jessica Oswald read hers first, followed by Reverend Ferguson, and then Bill Goodwin. The victim impact statements were sad and profound, relating the life of a daughter and how terribly she would be missed.

Reverend Ferguson's final words reflected how he viewed the loss of his daughter Cayla: "Her vibrancy and zest for life brightened my life whenever she was in my presence or whenever I thought about her. There will always be a great void for me and for her mother because she is no longer with us."

Bill Goodwin needed help to walk to the witness chair. It was provided by Garret Nelson. With a quivery voice, he read his statement with some difficulty. The courtroom was silent as everyone strained to hear every word.

"It's impossible for me to describe how much joy our Patti gave us. Throughout her short life, she was a child who was bright, outgoing, and personable. She was our only child. We gave her anything she wanted, but, surprisingly, she never wanted all that much. Even as a young child, she wanted to share her toys with others less fortunate. As a teenager, she was surrounded by friends who shared her values, good values. She finished first in her class at Collinsville High School because she worked hard, and she wanted, some day, to be a minister like her father. Once, she said that if that was not possible for any reason, she would just make a lot of money to support her parents in their old age. Yes, we could not have had a kinder, more compassionate daughter. Even as my Parkinson's disease progressed, she pretended not to notice while going out of her way to comfort me. Her mother and I will miss her terribly.

"It's primarily because of her compassion and her kindness to others that I want to make a recommendation to you, Your Honor, in her behalf. This man who took her life is not a bad man that I can see. He is only 28 years old, not terribly older than our beloved daughter. He, too, has a child that must be raised to be ambitious but kind, energetic but sharing, and successful while not forgetting those less fortunate around him. This child's father made a tragic mistake by using extremely poor judgment just one night in his life. We bear him no malice, but the law is correct in its position that there should be adequate punishment for such a horrible crime.

"My wife, Mary, and I have agonized about the degree of punishment that would be appropriate in this situation, even though we realize, Your Honor, that that decision is entirely yours. Nevertheless, we would like to suggest a sentence that would allow him to retake his life and to help reestablish a relationship with his only child. Perhaps ten years would be the right sentence, punishing him and yet allowing him to have a long, decent life after what would then be perhaps eight and a half years, a life that our Patti will never have. I ask this not in vengeance but in forgiveness because we feel that's what Patti would want. Thank you, Your Honor."

Many in the courtroom were stricken by Reverend Goodwin's words. A few moments later, they heard from Walter Caine. Many defendants at this juncture in a sentencing hearing will take the opportunity to apologize directly to the victims' family members. Some, certainly, hope that the judge will be impressed with their sometimes feigned sorrow to influence the judge's decision on prison time. Some are indeed sorry, but there might be some speculation as to whether the sorrow is being expressed to the victims or is really pity for their own unfortunate projected immediate future in prison. And some are truly remorseful for the consequences of their criminal action. This, no doubt, was the case with Walter Caine when he was given the opportunity by the judge to speak in his own behalf.

Many offenders carefully write out apologies and read them. Sometimes, they don't have the sense to turn and address the victims' families but merely read the document in a monotone, directly at the judge or looking down at notes, something to get through as quickly as possible. Walter Caine had no notes; he spoke from his heart.

"I can't express how terrible I feel and how sorry I am. I do not ask for forgiveness; I don't deserve forgiveness. I would never intentionally harm anyone, yet, in one unforgettable night, I drank in excess and drove a car in a way that would result in taking the lives of three wonderful young women and seriously injuring a fourth. I have no excuses for my behavior. If only I had died instead of them. If only I could make that awful night go away, I would in a heart beat. Instead, I'm standing here admitting that I've done something that was horrible beyond belief. I'm so sorry, I'm so sorry."

With this, the tears flowed from Walter Caine as well as from Betty and Ed Caine and even from a few parents of those young women who died unnecessarily and had the rest of their expected promising lives taken away from them.

Both the defense attorney, Norman Caswell, and State's Attorney John Blanchard argued briefly for what they thought would be an appropriate sentence for Walter Caine. Norman pointed out that Walter had never run afoul of the law, that he led an impeccable life, and that he was needed by his aging parents. He also pointed out that, if he could do so when he was released from prison or if he were to receive probation, he would offer to speak to others about the great dangers of drinking and driving. John Blanchard argued that drunk drivers who are responsible for deaths had to be severely punished. He told the judge that he needed to make an example of Walter Caine that would be noted by the community. He said that an exchange of 28 years in prison for causing deaths and injuries did not come remotely close to satisfying justice. Blanchard observed that, while a long prison term for Walter would be a hardship on his parents, Walter would still be alive, while the parents of Patti Goodwin, Maris Oswald, and Cayla Ferguson have lost their children forever.

Judge Byron Chase, like many judges, enjoyed his moment in the spotlight. Always a bit verbose when given an opportunity in the courtroom, there was no doubt that he would expound at length before pronouncing his sentence. He paused a few seconds, for effect, perhaps, or maybe to give the reporters in the room an opportunity to make pencils ready. Then again, perhaps he paused simply to gather his thoughts.

"I have been on the Bench now for almost 25 years," he began. "I may have never seen a matter before me that is so heart rending for those in attendance on either side of the courtroom. The crime that brings us all here today is a violent crime, as violent as an intentional taking of lives, because the result is the same. As a society, we have been battling the egregious sin of drunk driving for many years with very little success. As thousands of innocent people are killed year after year in this country by this senseless crime, we continue to struggle for ways to end this tsunami of evil. Our Legislature has increased the penalties at almost every session with very little success.

"A recent change in the law, however, may have some impact. It states that anyone who is responsible for a death as a result of drunk driving must – must – be imprisoned for a period of three to fourteen years. If there is more than one death as, sadly, in this case, the law requires a sentence of six to 28 years. The law does also say that probation is available for such crimes but only in extraordinary circumstances. I find no facts in this case that produce extraordinary circumstances. Consequently, a prison term is mandated.

"I want to express my deepest sympathies to the parents of the three young women who lost their lives and thank the parents who delivered such moving impact statements. As a judge, I wish that I had the power to restore them to their happier lives and give them their children back. Obviously, I can't do that. All I can do is punish the person who was responsible for this heinous crime.

"I've listened to and carefully considered the arguments made by the State's Attorney and by defense counsel. I've listened carefully to the individuals who were put on the stand by the prosecution in aggravation of the charges and by defense counsel in an attempt to mitigate the possible sentence. I've received letters of support for both the prosecutor's view and the defense's view. But, most of all, I've listened to the victim impact statements of the parents of the young women who have lost their lives. I am going to accept the recommendation of a victim's father and sentence Walter Caine to a period of ten years in the Department of Corrections with the knowledge that, with good behavior, he will be eligible for release in eight and a half years."

Judge Chase banged his gavel on the bench to end his pronouncement with judicial flourish.

Chapter Twelve

A good plaintiff lawyer follows the money if he has more than one possible defendant. Tom Lansing, of course, did exactly that. Armed now with a guilty plea in the criminal case and information resulting from his firm's investigation of certain Foster Ford practices, he filed a wrongful death action in behalf of the surviving relatives of the three Howard Christian College students who died so undeservedly and unnecessarily at the hands of a drunk driver, along with a personal injury suit in behalf of Heather.

Harry Foster, of course, panicked. Earlier, when he had received the call from Malcolm Collins, he had some hope that the lofty experience of this successful defense firm would provide a way out. Clearly, he was wrong. The news got worse when he met with Collins to discuss the case.

"I have ten million dollars of coverage," Harry said. "Will that cover the loss?"

Malcolm Collins was not a man to make rash responses. "We'll see. The suit is for twenty-five million as you know. I have no idea where this Thomas Lansing came up with that number, but we'll soon know."

"If they get that much, my business is down the drain. We'll be bankrupt. We can't pay out fifteen million dollars over and above my coverage."

"Mr. Foster, it is not my intention to have National Security pay out the first ten million. First, we are going to convince a jury that the fault lies with Walter Caine and Walter Caine alone. We need to demonstrate that your company is not in any way responsible for the crash. Caine's action was completely outside the scope of employment. His action was what is called a frolic, a foolish departure from his employment duties."

"Can you do that?" Harry asked.

"I think that there is very little chance that we can, so don't get your hopes up too much. What we have going for us, though, is our firm's experience, past success, and resources going up against a young man from Springfield, Illinois."

"I wouldn't underestimate him," Harry said.

"Because you're from Springfield?" Collins asked without expecting an answer.

If Malcolm Collins were to lecture a law school class on the doctrine of Respondeat Superior, he would say something like this: "The key to determining whether a principal may be liable for the torts of an agent under the doctrine of Respondeat Superior is whether the tort is committed within the scope of the agency or employment. The Restatement of Agency indicates the factors that today's courts will consider in determining whether a particular act occurred within the course and scope of employment. These factors are as follows: (1) Whether the employee's act was authorized, (2) The time, place, and purpose of the act, (3) Whether the act was one commonly performed by employees, (4) The extent to which the employer's interest was advanced by the act, (5) The extent to which the private interests of the employee were involved, (6) Whether the employer furnished the means or instrumentality, (7) Whether the employer had reason to know that the employee would do the act and whether the employee had ever done it before, and (8) Whether the act involved the commission of a serious crime."

Collins might also quote a Master-Servant case from 1834 – yes, 1834 – Joel v. Morison, which pointed out the difference between a mere detour from the employer's business, where the master would be responsible for the tort, and a "frolic on his own," where the master would not be liable.

"Anyway, Harry, we need to know about your operation here. Who gets to take cars home and how much did you or your supervisors know about this business of celebrating when your people met quotas? These are the twenty-five million dollar questions."

Harry was in a conundrum. In virtually all cases where individuals are sued – and they have liability insurance – they have no hesitation to allow the insurance company's paid gun to defend them. In so doing, they have a better lawyer than they could find on their own most likely, and there is no charge for the lawyer's services; in Harry's situation, the insurance company would be paying the entire damage award unless the recovery exceeded ten million. But now, there may be a possibility that his company would be liable for big bucks. Should he bring in his own lawyer? On the other hand, this guy Collins is good. Maybe the insurance company won't have to pay out ten million because Malcolm Collins will prove that Foster Ford is not liable. Then again, maybe this is the end of Foster Ford and the employment of Walter Caine's co-workers who drank with him in celebration that night. Maybe that, too, would be a part of a final justice.

Malcolm Collins' firm researched the law and a multitude of Respondeat Superior cases. Collins reached a conclusion. National Security would have to pay. His best tact now would be to outmaneuver the Springfield lawyer on how much his client would have to pay, so he scheduled a meeting. Tom Lansing had no fear of walking into the lion's den. He accepted Collins' invitation to meet with him in the Collins, Gunther, Price and Dean office in Boston.

"I thought that it would serve the interests of both of our clients if we had this preliminary get-together," Malcolm Collins said. "Thank you for coming."

"I'm always willing to help move a case along," Tom responded.

"I'm ready to recommend a reasonable offer to my client to end this litigation very early on. Why make the victims suffer any more than they have?"

"I'm listening," Tom said.

Collins sat back pensively. "Now, Tom ... Can I call you Tom?"

"Please do."

"Now, Tom, we both know that this twenty-five million is pipe dreaming. Let's look at the real monetary losses to the families. Can we do that?"

"I would be happy to hear your analysis," Tom replied.

"The typical successful college graduate could earn perhaps two million over a lifetime," Collins said. "And that's if they are very successful. Even without considering all other factors such as their gender and a lifetime of expenses, we are looking at maybe two point two million for each girl. The young lady who has incurred pain and suffering and may have expenses down the road – this young lady we would like to treat liberally. I think one point five million for her. That would be, let me see, six point six for the first three, another one point five. That's eight point one million. How does that sound coming right out of the box for a quick settlement?"

"Thank you for sharing your analysis," Tom said, "but here is what I believe can happen with this case. The young women were exceptionally bright and should have had a happy, lucrative future. Heather Sanford, who was so badly injured, was traumatized by the death of her three friends. We will have little difficulty proving vicarious liability on the part of Foster Ford. I think that I would like – I know I would like – to go to trial with this and let a jury decide on damages."

"Tom," Collins said, "I know that you're an ambitious young man and would like to enhance your reputation with a well-publicized trial. Believe me, we're not going to let you do that. We have accountants and actuaries who will spend weeks in front of the jury, if necessary, to demonstrate what damages really should be."

"Maybe," Tom said. "However, we're planning to point out to the jury the utter recklessness of a company that encourages its employees to party until they are drunk out of their minds and – and – give them cars to drive after they've done that. Can you spell punitive damages? I think we have a shot."

"You really do play hardball, don't you, Mr. Lansing?"
"No, no. I don't play at all, Mr. Collins," Tom said.

Tom Lansing may have been guilty of a bit of hyperbole when he talked of winning a twenty-five million dollar judgment. But, as lawyers tend to say, he had a good case. He had no aspirations, however, to close an important Springfield business, although he wondered if sending those partying employees scrambling for another job wouldn't be satisfying. What Tom had in mind was a settlement or a verdict that would result in National Security paying out the full ten million dollars of coverage and making Foster Ford pay a penalty that would mean reaching deep into the company's pockets without forcing the company to go bankrupt.

A clause in Foster Ford's contract with National Security stated that the insurance company had the obligation to defend its client, so Malcolm Collins had the duty to represent Foster Ford as well as the insurance company. Collins would have loved to settle this case for something less than ten million to save some insurance company money, but that possibility appeared dim. However, he was optimistic that he could accomplish something positive for Foster Ford. Before a second meeting with Tom Lansing, he visited with Harry Foster.

"Lansing is a sassy guy," Collins said to Harry Foster, "but I think his reach exceeds his grasp."

"And for me, that means what?" Harry asked.

"What if this suit costs you a half million dollars instead of the fifteen million that is Mr. Lansing's ridiculous objective?" Collins asked.

Harry cringed, but his interest was piqued. "It would be painful to have to pay out even that much, but, yeah, we could survive it."

"Maybe we could appeal to Lansing's sense of community. He's also smart enough to realize that a big judgment against your company would be simply uncollectible."

"Obviously," Harry said, "I want to pay out as little as possible. If you can get the five hundred thousand done, I guess I should consider myself lucky. Damn."

"That's an improvement over the eight point eight you floated," Tom Lansing said, "but I'm not free to accept that offer. You see, my clients have a number in mind as the absolute minimum; ten million, five hundred thousand isn't it. Foster Ford needs to be punished for the company's particularly dangerous behavior in essentially encouraging drinking and driving as a company fringe benefit."

"That's a bit extreme, Mr. Lansing. I think we can prove that management was not fully aware of the monthly festivities."

"They knew it wasn't a tea party," Tom said. "Look, I'm going to tell you what the number is that would satisfy the victims' families to the degree that they would finally put that night behind them."

"Yes?"

"It's eleven million, Mr. Collins," Tom said, "ten million from the insurance company and one million from Foster Ford."

"It will be difficult to sell this to Harry Foster, but I'll do what I can."

"Mr. Collins, I've investigated Foster Ford's financial status. I'm convinced that a million dollar contribution to the settlement of this action will hurt but is definitely do-able. Our offer is good to the end of the week."

Except for the Sanfords, who had a sudden need for money that exceeded Heather's medical costs, the victims' parents did not consider a multi-million dollar settlement to be a necessity. The pain of their losses was alleviated only slightly by the resolution of the criminal charges against Walter Caine. They, too, felt that Foster Ford had to be punished, if only financially, because of its disregard for the lives of others. Very early on, Tom Lansing had informed them that he thought that an eleven million dollar settlement was a distinct possibility. Consequently, they were not surprised to hear the news that a settlement had been reached for exactly that amount.

Chapter Thirteen

Yes, the Sanfords needed the money, money to settle a divorce action, replace lost income from sudden unemployment, and to pay lawyer fees for a criminal defense. However, these three categories did not follow in the logical sequence that one would imagine from events leading to this juncture.

First of all, there was Heather's revelation that she may have been sexually abused as a child by her own father. After this information was shared with one sister, Carrie, together they visited with older sister Elaine.

"Surely, this is some mental aberration resulting from the crash," Carrie said to Elaine with Heather satisfied to let Carrie do the talking. "Don't you think so, Elaine?"

Elaine was quiet for a moment, not hurrying her response. "No," she said simply.

"No? What are you saying, Elaine?" Carrie asked.

"I've been carrying this all of my life. I've been repressing it. He started with me!"

"I'm sorry, Elaine," Heather said. "I thought I was I wrong to think that it happened, but if it happened to you, too ..."

"I have this hazy memory of something that I've never been able to pin down," Elaine said. "I've never been able to fathom what it was all about, only that it was horribly wrong and it involved Dad. We can't both be imagining it, can we?"

"We've all heard and read about this kind of thing," Heather said. "I thought that it was some freakish impact on my brain because of the crash."

"Let's fact it," Elaine said. "If we both think it happened, it must have happened."

"What are we going to do?" Heather said almost pleadingly.

"We have to tell Mom. She should know," Carrie said.

"We know that they hardly can stand each other now," Elaine said. "What will Mom do? She'll kill him."

"Nevertheless, she should know," Elaine concluded. "We know that he's done some other things that she didn't know about until much later. I don't think that we should keep this a secret from her."

Ann Sanford did not take this news well. She tried so hard to keep the marriage together for the sake of her daughters. Divorce was only a way out for the young, she thought. She knew, of course, of his other sexual proclivities, but she had been under the assumption that that was over. Now, the news that his peculiar sexual activity had begun so early in their marriage and consisted of such abnormal behavior was just too much. She confronted him.

"Now, I know why we have not had a marriage in anything but name for so long," she told Paul Sanford.

"What is it now?" he groused. "Whatever it is, get over it."

"I put up with your seeing other women because I never found out about them until the affairs were over, and you always promised that they wouldn't happen again."

"For Pete's sake," Paul growled, "why are you rehashing things that happened years ago?"

"Yes, years ago," Ann said. "Years ago you violated our own daughters. Don't try to deny it."

Clearly, Sanford was astonished at what his wife had said. For a moment, he was speechless. His mind was racing on how to respond to this sudden accusation.

"You can't put that on me. I will deny it. That's insane."

"Yes, it's insane. You're insane. You should have sought help long ago," Ann screamed.

"This accusation is insane," Sanford said. "You're making this up to cover up your own behavior. I've seen you talking to the guy next door. Always friendly, aren't you? Maybe too friendly. I'm not taking your insults any more. Listen to me and listen good. You need help, psychiatric help."

"You're not going to manipulate me like that any more. You think that you can do anything you want. Not this time. I'm leaving you, Paul. I've thought about it often. This time, I'm going to do it."

"Leave!" Sanford said. "Just leave. There's no way that we should have stayed together this long. You have one crazy, ridiculous idea after another. Your accusation this time has just gone too far."

"You've always done exactly what you wanted to do, without regard for me or our daughters. I'm disgusted with you," she shouted.

Ann screamed at him from less than a foot away. She was literally in his face. Often, they had had intense arguments. Each time, Paul stormed from the room or punched a wall or slammed a door to vent his frustrations. He had never hit her, although he often visualized doing so. But now, she was thoroughly invading his space. He could no longer restrain himself. He had to make her stop talking; he lashed out with a fist. He struck her hard in the face and, once that fist blow was struck, his pent-up anger worsened. He struck her again across the face with the back of his hand. Ann fell to the floor.

Heather had been in her bedroom with the door closed, not wanting to hear the argument that she knew would ensue, but then she became aware that the shouting was getting louder. Then she heard the sound of flesh upon flesh and realized that the arguing had turned to physical violence. She ran to her parents' room and saw her father standing over her mother with his hand still raised as though he was about to inflict another blow.

There are approximately 700,000 documented incidents of domestic violence each year in this country. In addition to physical abuse, there are many other forms of abuse that often lead to physical abuse: verbal, sexual, emotional, economic, and spiritual. Physical abuse, however, is most prevalent. In the center of any form of abuse is power and control; the abuser will use coercion, threats, intimidation, isolation, blame – all to exercise power and control over his or her partner.

Often, there are clear signs of trouble before the abuse takes place, but these are
often ignored by the partner who wants to be loved and appreciated. Signs that lead to eventual abuse include jealousy, attempts to control behavior, quick involvement, unfair expectations, isolation, and extreme sensitivity.

Ann had witnessed the signs on multiple occasions but always believed Sanford when he begged for her forgiveness, and she believed him when he made promises that his anger and cheating incidences would never happen again.

"Dad, don't!" Heather screamed.

For a moment, time froze, then Heather ran from the room. Sanford turned in disgust.

Heather, now still in pain from her injuries, was further agonized by her father's actions. She made the call to the local police. Two young police officers arrived to investigate a domestic disturbance, not uncommon for them and fellow officers.

"This is none of your concern," Paul shouted at them after Heather had let the policemen in.

"Sir, we need to find out what's going on," one of the policemen said.

"This is between me and my wife. That's it," Sanford said.

"Ma'am," the other police officer said, "Are you all right?"

Ann obviously wasn't. She was holding a wet cloth to her face. "No, I'm not," she said. "My husband has battered me."

"You bitch. You don't know what battering is," Sanford screamed.

"Sir, I think that you should come with us," said the first policeman. "We'll straighten this out at the station."

"Get out of my house," Sanford hollered. "Get the hell out!"

That same policeman walked toward Sanford with handcuffs in his hand. "You're coming with us."

As he approached Sanford, he was met with a wild attempt by Sanford to land a blow on the officer's face. His attempted punch barely grazed the policeman's cheek, but, in an instant, the younger, trained policeman had Sanford's hands behind him in handcuffs.

Chapter Fourteen

Danielle Ferguson couldn't believe her ears. The Reverend Douglas Ferguson called her not for lunch but for dinner. They met in a very nice restaurant on the outskirts of Trenton, Le Maison. She had heard nothing but good things about the food and the service from her administrative secretary, who seemed to know all about the good restaurants. How she kept her 110-pound, curvaceous figure was a complete mystery to Danielle, considering the woman's penchant for frequenting only the best restaurants.

"Is this a date?" Danielle asked, not very seriously.

"Do you want it to be one?" Douglas asked.

"Sure, why not?" Danielle responded. "We've been quite civil with each other now for over twenty years. I know that Cayla was the reason, but you've always been a decent man, Douglas."

"Remember when you used to call me Dougie?"

Danielle laughed. "Not for long. The first time that I saw you in that dark suit and collar, I knew that I could never call you Dougie again. Even Doug was a stretch. No, you're Douglas."

"Well, I never called you Dannie, although that might have been fun. Danielle Ferguson, CEO. That's your name."

"How are you doing, Douglas? Does it still hurt, I mean, Cayla?"

"It's been hard … for both of us," Douglas said, "but I've accepted that it was God's will. Surely, she has brightened up Heaven."

"Thank you for giving me that thought," Danielle said. "It's comforting. You know, someone did a study on the effect of marital relationships after a couple lost a child in an accident. I have no idea why anyone would pursue a project like that, but the study indicated that a large number of marriages just can't hold up after the experience, something like thirty per cent."

"That may be accurate," Douglas replied, "but I feel certain that such a tragedy must have brought parents closer together in many cases. How could it not? They need each other, because no outsider could possible understand their feelings."

"I know I'll always need you as my understanding ex-husband. I'm grateful that we can be this close after all the years that we've been apart."

"Have you ever thought about remarrying, Danielle?" Douglas asked. "I know that your company hardly gives you time to breathe, must less provide the time to find a new husband."

"Sure, I've thought about it. Leaving a boardroom full of people and coming home to an empty condo is occasionally depressing. That's one reason it was so great to have Cayla's visits. Of course, I'll miss her in many other ways. She certainly grew on me, even though I was an absentee mother."

"We'll both miss her, that's certain," Douglas said, "but we have each other, even if only occasionally, to remind us that she was with us in this life even if for such a short time."

"We will," Danielle agreed. "I must tell you, Douglas, that this has made me re-think my life in some ways. Would it surprise you if I told you that I'm growing wary of the traveling, the pressures, and the fourteen to sixteen-hour days?"

"Yes, it would. You are a finely honed apparatus for a human being. I can't imagine you not being a hard-driving CEO."

"Success doesn't always bring happiness is an old cliché," Danielle said. "All of a sudden, I'm realizing how true that is."

"You're not thinking of resigning, are you?"

"I've given it some thought. It may be time for a change in my life," Danielle said. "How about you, Douglas, will your life go on as it has been? You're a busy guy yourself."

"Yes, my conviction is even greater now," Douglas responded. "Right after we lost Cayla, I was having some doubts, but I have a wonderful congregation. I received overwhelming support from everyone when they heard the bad news. Many that I counseled in tough times became my counselors. No, I'm going to stay and just keep going."

"And, since you asked me that question, I'll ask you. Have you ever thought of remarrying? I'm sure that you have had opportunities."

"No, I think that our oil and water careers discouraged me. I would only fear that it would happen all over again."

"I'm in town next week. What would you say to a home-cooked meal? Well, I do have a live-in employee who prepares my meals for me when I'm here, but it's technically home-cooked. Maybe we could get to know each other a bit better. We didn't try that hard way back when. What do you think?"

"It's a date," Douglas said.

Life in the Oswald family had changed considerably also. The four girls who survived Maris saw their future prospects brighten because of the money due the family from the settlement. Henry and Jessica would always miss their unannounced favorite daughter who lost her life in a car crash at the age of twenty. They had no thoughts of improving their personal lives with their shares of the windfall – no new home or cars. Their money would be used to benefit their daughters in any way required. That was their pledge.

In fact, some of the money already belonged to the daughters. Understandably, Maris had no will. Under the laws of their state, the money would go in equal shares to Henry, Jessica, and the four girls, although the shares of the younger girls would go in a trust until they attained the age of eighteen. Mary, Margaret, Marsha, and Madeline – yes, all names beginning with the letter M – would use the money well. Mary, the oldest, had recently married. Her newly acquired wealth would support a new business venture, a day care facility aptly named The Maris Day Care Center. Margaret had always dreamed of medical school but never revealed that dream so as not to put financial stress on her parents. Now a recent graduate of a Nursing School, she applied and was admitted to Southern Illinois Medical School.

Marsha, the only teenager in the family at fourteen, would have her share placed in trust as would six-year-old Madeline.

"I'm never going to spend a penny of that money," Marsha announced one day. "It's not fair that Maris had to die to make us all wealthy."

"I'm sure that Maris would have wanted you to have a good education," Jessica said. "None of us wanted money obtained in this way. That's why we should honor Maris by spending the money wisely."

"I'm going to give mine away to charity," Madeline said. "I don't need money. I'm going into the convent as soon as I graduate from high school."

"Last week, you were going to be a veterinarian," Margaret said. "The week before that, you wanted to be a ballet dancer."

"Don't make fun of me," warned the feisty six-year old.

"Maybe she's smarter than all of us," Marsha said. "Maybe we should be thinking of a charity for most of the money. Maybe one of those organizations that tries to prevent drunk driving."

"I'm sure that Americans Against Intoxicated Drivers could use a contribution," Jessica said, "but let's not get carried away quite yet."

Reverend Ferguson began to wonder how it would look to his congregation if a single woman moved in with him. She was, after all, once his wife. Then, he realized just how ridiculous that thought was. Still, they had become very close in the last few months, especially since Danielle had become a former CEO.

It was at another dinner suggested by Douglas that the conversation became serious.

"I think we know," began Douglas, "why our marriage ended and why we have had a good relationship despite that all these years."

"Yes," answered Danielle, "there is no doubt that we went each our own way because we were two very busy people with interests that were vastly different."

"You know, if it weren't for that important job of yours, you would have made a marvelous wife for a minister. You could have helped in so many ways with your leadership and organization skills."

"I suppose," Danielle replied, "but we had such different ambitions. There I was with my MBA from Harvard and there you were with your Divinity degree. We got the most out of our degrees, didn't we?"

"We did," Douglas agreed.

"But look, Douglas, I don't believe we ever hated or even disliked each other as so many divorced people do. Sure, we stayed friendly primarily because we shared a wonderful daughter, but there was more to it than that, wasn't there?"

"All of a sudden, our lives have changed enormously," Douglas pointed out. "Naturally, our loss of Cayla was devastating, but now here you are a retired CEO. At the same time, I find myself older, unfortunately, but ably assisted by two wonderful new ministers so that my need to succeed is no longer of such paramount importance."

"So here we are," Danielle said, "two people who still admire each other, with time to devote to making our relationship something more important."

"I've never stopped loving you," Douglas said.

"Those were the words I wanted to hear," Danielle said.

So he did the right thing: He asked Danielle to marry him, to live the rest of their lives together. Money was certainly not a consideration; they had received their shares of the settlement. However, he didn't think that it was right to keep it all. After she said yes to his second proposal to her in twenty-two years, he suggested that they give some of the money to a worthy cause, perhaps Americans Against Intoxicated Drivers. The CEO in her said no.

Chapter Fifteen

Under the current leadership of Jack Northrup, AAID indeed could use contributions. The organization had been formed in the Eighties by two women who had been victimized by drunk drivers. The organization had laudatory goals, initially. The primary efforts included education, victim advocacy, and lobbying for tougher laws to combat the national problem. Very rapidly, the organization grew with chapters in each state. Most state chapters formed local chapters.

The organization was quite successful for the first twenty-five years or so because victims of intoxicated drivers and their families participated in providing services on a volunteer basis. They did so without compensation, receiving travel expenses only. In addition, the organization somehow had the ability to recruit outstanding staff members for very little compensation. Somehow, along the way, however, things went awry.

The great mistake, apparently, was when the organization decided to improve the quality of its national staff by recruiting from other companies at much higher salaries. From there, it was all downhill. First, the high paid staff, with no real feeling for the plight of victims or the problems of intoxicated driving, decided that the national organization needed to assume more control over state chapters. This was accomplished by eliminating local chapters and setting up regional offices to be run by a new kind of director, one experienced not in victim services, lobbying, or education but in fund raising.

"We need," Northrup said to the hapless, clueless staff, "more and better fundraising by the state chapters. We're going broke. Any suggestions?"

The ideas coming from the staff members were not particularly ingenious:

"Cut back victim services."

"Better not do that. We're not providing much in the way of services as it is," Northrup said.

"Recruit victim volunteers to assume the duties of paid victim advocates."

"We might be able to do that," Northrup said. "There are a number of victims who have helped and others who have expressed an interest in helping. Trouble is, though, we'd have to set up training seminars for them. We can't leave that to the states. Maybe we'd better have training here in Dallas or in some other big city and have people on the national staff do the training. That's a possibility."

"No longer pay travel expenses for volunteers."

"You know, that might work. The volunteers don't put in for expenses sometimes anyway. If they really want to volunteer, maybe they would be willing to incur the expenses involved in volunteering. It might be a way to separate the really valuable volunteers from the others."

"Eliminate all lobbying at the state level. Instead, form a paid group of staff members to work with Congress to get national legislation."

"Hmmm. Most of our state directors really don't have a clue about how to lobby, anyway. They're fund raisers. Some of these people used to spend more time at their capitols than in the trenches taking in contributions. Let's explore that one."

"Charge for educational services."

"Why not? The schools have money to spend, don't they? Why should the teachers get paid while we work for nothing? Good thought."

"Charge for victim services."

"Maybe. Everybody else charges for services. Why not us? Lawyers make a ton on victims; why should we provide free services? Of course, we have a history of not charging, but maybe we can figure out how to get by that juggernaut."

Northrup weighed the recommendations. "All of these ideas are worth considering, but I have another thought."

Of course, the staff waited breathlessly for this idea.

"Even though we have provided advice and advocacy only in criminal cases, there have been many civil suits that have produced large monetary awards for victims and their families. Why can't we tap into some of that?"

One member of the staff had actually been around for a few years. "We don't normally ask for contributions from victims that we have helped, at least we haven't until now."

Another staff member had a related recommendation. "Or we could try to get major contributions from the law firms that handled the cases."

"Okay, this has been a good meeting," said Northrup. "Let's go get 'em."

That should have been the beginning of the end for AAID, but, unfortunately, it was not. Although most local chapter volunteers were pained to be dismissed from local activity because of the elimination of their chapters, some continued to be involved with the organization because they realized that the policy decisions coming from the national staff were inane, but they believed in the original goals and objectives.

AAID Executive Director Northrup followed through with his idea of tapping into victims and victims' estates. He was standing near assistant Don Dolittle's desk.

"Can you get me the names of all victims and beneficiaries of successful civil suits against drunk drivers?" Northrup asked Dolittle.

"Whew, tall order," Dolittle said. "We'd have to check county records one by one all over the country, I suppose."

"How about if we get all of the state chapters involved. We have a fundraiser at each chapter, don't we?" Northup asked.

"Sure. In most cases, it's the fundraiser who heads up the state chapter."

"Let's lean on them to get some info to us pronto," Northrup said.

"It's as good as done."

"Wait a minute!" Northrup said. "Let me do a quick check of my emails. I think there's something from Illinois that I didn't look at yesterday … Yep, here it is. There was an eleven-million-dollar settlement in Springfield. That's near Chicago, isn't it?"

"No-o-o. Actually, I think it's about two hundred miles from Chicago," Dolittle said.

"Right," Northrup agreed. "It is the capital, though, right? Or is Chicago the capital?"

"I think it depends on which politician you ask," Dolittle commented.

"Let's make some contacts. Tell them all what we're doing for victims of crashes like theirs. Tell them we need money to keep operating."

"That's a little cold, isn't it?" Dolittle asked. "I mean, contacting people so soon after they've lost someone to a drunk driving crash."

"Naw," answered Northrup. "They'll only blow the money some other way."

Chapter Sixteen

Walter Caine certainly was not comfortable in his new surroundings. The adjustment was difficult. Prisoner Number 5416 hassled him from the beginning, calling him the college kids killer. As prisons go, though, this was a good one as far as security and administration. Consequently, there was deliberation in placement and movement of prisoners. For that reason, and because Walter was college educated, he drew the librarian job.

The warden, Gary Watkins, was sympathetic to Walter's plight for a personal reason. Five years before, he and two assistants attended a retirement party for a senior staff member. Both of his assistants drank liberally. The warden drank conservatively but foolishly got into the car with one of the assistants doing the driving. Watkins was in the back seat and watched in horror as the car plummeted off the road, failing to maneuver a slight curve in the road. The crash knocked him unconscious. He was fortunate in that he suffered only slight injuries. The assistant in the passenger seat was killed, however. The driver was charged and found guilty of Aggravated DUI resulting in a death. Paradoxically, he was serving a three-year sentence in Watkins' prison.

Except for that lapse of not exercising common sense, Watkins was probably one of the best wardens in the country. One of his practices was to meet with each prisoner shortly after the prisoner's arrival. Consequently, he met with Walter Caine.

"You're going to be with us for quite a while," Warden Watkins said. "You'll have to make the best of it. Stay out of trouble the best you can and just put the time in. That's the only advice I have for you. Do you have any questions?"

"As you know," Walter said, "I'm here because I was responsible for deaths and injuries, all as a result of driving drunk."

"Yes, I realize that you're not an axe murderer and don't want to be treated like one, but the Corrections system doesn't discern between you and that other guy."

"I know that," Walter replied. "I'm not asking for any different treatment. I committed a terrible crime and now I'm paying for it. What I really want to talk to you about is the possibility of doing more, not less."

Watkins hadn't heard anything unusual in these recent arrival interviews in a number of years. His interest piqued. "What do you mean?"

"I want to do more, much more than just serve time," Walter said. "There are still thirteen thousand to seventeen thousand people in this country killed by people like me. Somehow, I want to be active now to combat the problem."

"Interesting thought," Watkins said. "What do you have in mind, specifically?"

Walter reflected a moment. "I've been assigned to the library, which I appreciate. This might give me an opportunity to do some research. What I really would like to do is communicate with the outside, maybe write some newspaper or magazine articles."

"And the message you would be sending would be …?"

"Whether the articles are based on research or my own experience, they would always demonstrate the enormous dangers involved in drinking and driving. It didn't get through to me, and many others apparently aren't listening."

"Do you have the necessary writing skills?" the warden asked.

"I've been a writer all my life," Walter answered. "I just fell into the financial manager job because that was available to me and it paid really well. The fact is that I'm a better writer than a financial manager. English was my college degree."

"Communicating freely with the outside would be extraordinary," Watkins said. "I would have to see everything you write before it left here. You know that, don't you?"

"Absolutely. I would want any suggestions that you might want to make, also. I have to tell you that it didn't take very long for other prisoners to tell me about your personal experience with a drunk driving crash. You understand the problem."

"Let me sleep on it," the warden said. "It's an appealing idea, but it's so unorthodox that I have to give it careful consideration."

Gary Watkins decided that he would let Walter do some writing, as long as he would carefully review all articles. The first of Walter's articles was an op-ed in the Chicago Tribune:

LET'S GET SERIOUS ABOUT THE DUI PROBLEM
Walter Caine*

It's really time to stop pussyfooting around with a problem that kills over 13,000 people in this country each year and injures a half million people. Let's get serious and have legislation that will truly be effective to stop this carnage on the streets and highways.

The killing and maiming of victims of drunk driving crashes has to come to an end, and the only way to accomplish that is through truly meaningful, effective legislation. We have an opportunity for Illinois to lead the way, to show the nation how to put a stop to this senseless crime.

I am calling on members of the Legislature, the Illinois Secretary of State, the Illinois Department of Transportation, and organizations such as Americans Against Intoxicated Drivers to support a bold, new, necessary step to eliminate deaths and injuries as the result of drunk driving.

My personal experience has convinced me that a giant step needs to be taken if we are ever going to protect our citizens from the dangers on our roads caused by drunk drivers.

Let's face it. We've tried to deal with the problem and failed. Drunk drivers apparently are not all that concerned about fines and possible jail time. Knowing that supervision is virtually a lock for a first-time offender minimizes the seriousness of the crime. A loss of a driver's license is usually short-term. The law builds in great reluctance to take a license away. And when it does happen, often the individual simply drives without one.

Specifically, my proposal is that the Legislature enact laws that would provide that:

1. All convicted drunk drivers (driving with a blood alcohol content of .08 or more) would lose their licenses forever – lifetime revocation.

2. Anyone convicted of driving without a license that has been revoked for a drunk driving conviction after the effective date of the new law would forfeit the vehicle to the state.

3. While supervision for a first-time DUI charge would still be possible, all such first time offenders receiving supervision would be required to attend a Victim Impact Panel to insure not only that such offenders would recognize the dangers they imposed through drunk driving but would be informed of the penalty of lifetime revocation upon conviction of the next DUI or violation of supervision on the initial DUI.

Victim Impact Panels are presentations in which DUI offenders are ordered by the court to listen to victims relate how a drunk driver affected their families through loss of a family member or through serious injuries. Victim Impact Panels are presented regularly throughout the state by Victim Impact Speakers and numerous Probation Departments and State's Attorneys' offices, as well as by other organizations such as Americans Against Intoxicated Drivers, Mothers Against Drunk Driving, and the Alliance Against Intoxicated Motorists.

Please join me in writing to your State Senators and Representatives to demand that we get drunk drivers off the roads by enacting new, tougher legislation.

 *Walter Caine is a prisoner who is serving ten years for Aggravated DUI. He was responsible for the death of three college students when he drove drunk on the wrong side of a highway.

Ed and Betty Caine would be allowed to see Walter twice a month, and they would do their best to get to the prison at every opportunity, but one visit resulted in Walter learning some disturbing news.
 "How are they treating you, Son?" Betty asked.
 "It's not so bad, Mom. There are some tough-acting individuals in here, no question about that, but the guards are very alert. I'm enjoying my work in the library. That gives me a great deal of time to do some writing. The warden has been very good to me."
 "I saw your newspaper column," Ed said. "You laid it right out there."
 "We're very proud of you, Walter," Betty said, "for making the best of your situation. Hopefully, people will read and heed your advice."
 "Read and heed, huh, Mom," Walter said. "That's good. Maybe you should be writing."

Betty laughed at this. "I'm so pleased that you're dealing with this terrible imprisonment so well."

"I'm going to do my best," Walter said. "Of course, I would rather not be here. Most of all, I would rather that I never drank and drove that night. … Don't worry about me, Mom and Dad; you guys taught me to persevere."

"We have some news that you may not welcome," Ed said.

"What's wrong?" Walter asked.

"Debby left us a message on our answering machine," Betty said. "I think she waited until we were at church Sunday morning so she wouldn't have to talk to us directly."

"Is there a problem with Johnny?"

"No, no," Betty answered. "Johnny's fine. You know he spends every Wednesday with us. He's a great kid."

"What was the message, Mom?"

"She told us she got married to a guy named Todd somebody, got married in Las Vegas last weekend. The divorce from you was final only a few days before that, I think," Walter's mother said.

"So you don't know anything about this man?" Walter asked.

"I made a few calls," Ed said. "You know that she went back to work at that restaurant where you met her. I knew a few people there so I asked them what they knew."

"All I care about is that she married someone who's going to be good to Johnny," Walter said.

"That's what I'm a little worried about," Ed said. "The man's been married three times before. He's got kids here and there. I don't think there's a concern about his maltreating Johnny; he may not care whether Johnny exists or not."

"They're still going to let Johnny come over every Wednesday, aren't they?" Walter asked.

"They had better or they're going to get an argument from me," Ed said. "Debby would probably let him come over more often, I don't know. Want me to find out?"

"Yeah," Walter said. "That would be great. Maybe you can bring him here once in a while."

"Right now, he doesn't know you're here, Walter," Betty said. "Early on, Debby left us a message that she doesn't want Johnny to know that you are in prison. I just didn't want to tell you that."

"What does he think?" Walter asked.

Betty was concerned that Walter wouldn't like the report. "She told him that you had a medical condition that would keep you away for a long time. She told us she would tell him the truth when he was older."

"I don't know if I should be relieved or angry," Walter said. "I guess it's just as well that he doesn't see me like this for now. I can't believe he won't find out, though, sooner or later, maybe from other kids who hear their parents talking about it."

"As soon as he does, we'll talk to him if you want. Then, maybe he can come to see you," Ed said.

"In the meantime," Walter said, "Debby's probably right. No need to let my son know that I am a drunk who killed three people."

Walter was prolific. The articles flowed from the prison but always through Gary Watkins. After eight submissions had been printed in newspapers and magazines, there was definitely an interest in the prisoner of Centralia Correctional Center, for each article explained who the author was, a prisoner serving ten years for Aggravated DUI because he was responsible for the death of three college students when he drove drunk on the wrong side of a highway.

The articles were published by regional newspapers and by magazines with few subscribers. However, a reporter with Time Magazine ran across one of the articles when he was preparing a piece on driving under the influence. From there, he found Walter's other efforts. This, he thought, might interest an editor. And so it was that Time editor Mike Loudon set up a meeting with warden Gary Watkins and asked if Walter Caine could be present at the meeting.

"We're working on a comprehensive analysis of issues involving intoxicated driving. Even with the newer concerns of distracted driving, primarily text messaging by young people and unwise cell phone use, we don't want the dangers of intoxicated driving to be forgotten. It's still a clear and present danger to drink and drive."

"You're looking at the choir," Warden Watkins said, "so, no need to preach about those dangers to us."

"I know, but I wanted you both to know what we have in mind and get a commitment from you," Loudon said. "We'd like to feature both of you in an article and include some of Mr. Caine's work, maybe give him a platform for some additional material."

"What do you think, Walter?" Watkins said.

"Of course, I would like to participate as long as we're getting the right ideas across. Is it possible for me to do this, Mr. Watkins?"

"I'll want to talk to my superiors before I can agree to participate," Watkins said. "As for your participation, well, I think I've already opened those floodgates, so it's up to you, Walter."

Loudon broke in. "There will be compensation involved for your efforts. I'm assuming that Mr. Caine can not profit by his work. Isn't that correct?"

"Yes, it is," Watkins said. "No question about that. And if I participate, I feel that I shouldn't profit by my efforts either."

"That's what we thought. We were thinking of a contribution to a charity in your names," Loudon said. "Or maybe the State of Illinois would accept a grant for the improvement of the prison library, perhaps, or for exercise equipment, something along those lines. Maybe a contribution to AAID if you would prefer."

"Any of the above might work," the warden said.

"I don't know how much money you mean," Walter said, "but I wonder if we couldn't look into a monument to the Christian Howard students there off the highway, where it all shouldn't have happened."

"Why don't I look into what the State would allow us to do," Watkins said. "Except for that small detail, and checking with my bosses, I think you might have a deal."

As Editor Loudon left, Warden Gary Watkins had one caution for prisoner Walter Caine: "So far, so good, Walter, but don't forget that you're a convicted felon and will continue to be treated like one until your release. Don't let the Time exposure go to your head. Tomorrow, you might be in charge of cleaning restrooms."

Chapter Seventeen

Although it was by far the most embarrassing moment of his life, the arrest of Paul Sanford may have been the turnaround he needed. Upon release from the county jail after thirty days, he was required to obtain psychiatric care, go to an anger control workshop, and stay away from his family because of a temporary order of protection. He learned a great deal about himself in his sessions with a psychiatrist, including determining exactly why he had such disrespect for women. Basically, it seems, his problem emanated from experiences he had as a child that involved a friend's father who used to brag to both his son and Paul about his prowess with women. The man, who was long divorced, was paradoxically proud of his collection of posters and photographs of scantily clad women and pornographic videos. That man needed psychiatric care, but it was Paul Sanford who eventually received those services.

The workshop on anger control was highly successful once Sanford recognized that his anger was fueled by life-long guilt and a failure to understand normal male-female relationships. It was miraculous, really, that he conceived such outstanding daughters. The order of protection was eventually dismissed, and Paul reestablished communications with his wife first by phone and then in person.

"I can't begin to tell you," Sanford began, "how much I regret my behavior for so many years. The promiscuity was unforgivable."

"How can I possibly believe that you have now changed from the man I've known for so long?" Ann asked.

"I can't expect you to understand the revelation I've had about myself that came through the psychiatric help I've had during the past few months."

"The girls and I have grown quite accustomed to not having you here," Ann said. "Despite everything, though, Heather made the decision to finance your criminal defense and your professional help. As you well know, the money from the settlement has been paid, and all of it belongs to Heather."

"I've talked to my former employer. I've convinced him to take me back. He was very understanding of what I've been through."

"That's good news," Ann said. "I want you to straighten your life out if you possibly can. If your unfaithfulness was due to some mental aberration, and if you are indeed free of that problem, I wish you well. But I don't think I can forgive you for what you did to Elaine and Heather when they were so young."

"I deserve your condemnation for my seeing other women and for the way I treated you, but I still deny that I was guilty of the kind of things you believe I did when those girls were small. I don't understand the accusations at all."

Physically, Heather was making great strides toward returning to the healthy young woman she was before the crash. Her mind was another matter. She had occasional migraines and an odd combination of short and long-term memory lapses. Her doctor assured her that time – and some medication – would eventually be the cure-all. A nagging problem inherent in the memory puzzle was the mystery of whether her recollection of events involving her father was actually accurate. She met with Elaine.

"This is crazy, Elaine," Heather said, "but ... I just don't know how to tell you this."

"What's wrong, Heather?"

"I think I'm responsible for all of Dad's problems."

"What are you talking about, Heather? He was cheating on Mom, he punched Mom and tried to punch a cop, and he took liberties with us when we were just children. How are you responsible for any of that?"

Heather was clearly reluctant to say what was on her mind. "Maybe that thing with Dad didn't happen after all, at least not with me."

"What? Are you serious?" exclaimed Elaine. "What do you mean? You remembered it!"

"I … I thought I did, but then I remembered this book I read and then I was confused and then I couldn't remember and then I remembered Dad hugging me and then it was all mixed up. Then you said you had the same experience, and all of a sudden, I was convinced again, and … I don't think he did it."

"And now you're wondering if my memory was working right," Elaine said. "God, I don't know. He was always very affectionate to us. When I heard what you remembered, I somehow believed I had a repressed memory similar to yours. No, I'm sure … No, I'm not sure."

Heather was beside herself. "If we hadn't been so sure that it happened, we wouldn't have told Mom, and she wouldn't have accused him, and he wouldn't have hit her, and he wouldn't have tried to hit the cop and gone to jail."

Heather and her sister fell into each other's arms and had an enormous cry. Maybe it was all for the best, however. After all, Paul Sanford was now a new man. Or was he?

Heather and Elaine Sanford wrote a joint letter to their father, which they shared with their mother and with their sister Carrie. The letter was full of apologies but also with uncertainties. The entire family was in turmoil. Paul Sanford called each of them and said that he understood, and he begged their forgiveness for all of his past behavior, saying that their suppositions were unfortunate but not disastrous. He was ready to move on with his life, he said.

Ann, however, seized the opportunity to go through with the divorce proceedings that she had initiated. Although she sympathized with Paul's predicament, she simply had enough. She, also, wanted to move on.

"Nothing will ever be the same," Carrie lamented.

"I'll never forgive myself," Heather said. "If those terrible ideas hadn't somehow formed in my brain, we would still have parents who are together."

"Please don't blame yourself, Heather," Elaine said. "After all that you've been through, you were entitled to make a mistake. Most importantly, it wasn't your mistake that caused the divorce. Mom and Dad have been feuding forever."

"And," Carrie joined in, "Dad has always been tyrannical. Your accusations, real or not, simply brought his real personality to the forefront."

"What now?" Heather asked.

"I don't know about you guys, but I'm going to support Mom as much as I can," Elaine said. "I'm going to worry about Dad later."

"I think it's up to him to mend fences," Carrie added. "I'm with you, Elaine. We need to make sure Mom's okay."

"Of course, I agree," Heather said, "but Dad isn't holding any grudges against me. He calls me every few days to make sure I'm still doing all right."

"It's not my business," Elaine said, "but you gave him quite a lot of money to get through his problems, didn't you?"

"Sure," Heather answered. "I don't need all the money that I received in the crash settlement. He's still family, so if he needs money or if you guys or Mom need some money, I have it. Of course, I'll be using some of the money to continue school."

"Just take care of yourself with that money," advised Elaine. "Put it in a safe place in case you need it in the future. You've been through so much, and I don't know if you've fully recovered yet."

"I know," Heather said. "My memory is still not quite dependable, as we know. I'll tell you, though, that Dad has offered to help me with keeping the money safe. He knows a lot about investments."

Chapter Eighteen

Not everyone was satisfied with Judge Byron Chase's decision to sentence Walter Caine to ten years in prison. Many thought that the sentence was too light considering the possible range of six years to twenty-eight years for multiple deaths due to drunk driving. The Fergusons thought that the sentence was minimal, knowing that they had lost their daughter and that the man responsible for her death would only lose a possible eight and a half years of freedom. Paul Sanford, of course, was upset. He blamed the smaller sentence for part of his woes. The Oswalds accepted the sentence without rancor because that's how they were. The Goodwins, of course, were satisfied because the idea of a ten-year sentence came from Bill Goodwin. Many others, however, in the press, in law enforcement, in victim advocacy, and in the State's Attorney's office, thought that Caine should have received a sentence that was much closer to the maximum. One local newspaper editorial pointed out other sentences that had been meted out in the last few years for drunk driving deaths: Twenty-six years for killing four members of a family in White County; fourteen years for a single death, because the offender had some prior DUIs, in Champaign County; four years for being responsible for a passenger's death in Franklin County. The editorial pointed out that if four years was appropriate in the last mentioned case, at least twelve years should be a sentence for three deaths. Most remarkable, said the editorial, was the sentence of a man in Champaign County to ten years in prison not for killing anyone but for crashing into a police squad car, primarily based on prior convictions of robbery, theft, driving under the influence, and driving under revocation. The ten-year sentence given to Caine, claimed the editorial writer, did not match up. A number of letters to the editor agreed with the editorial.

None of this escaped the attention of Judge Byron Chase, despite the fact that he was contemplating retiring from the Bench. He agonized about it primarily because he wanted to be remembered for his many wise decisions, not for the last felony case that he heard that resulted in an unpopular sentence. He and John Blanchard discussed it over a few cold ones at the Bar Association's annual golf outing when no one else was present.

"What ever happened to judicial discretion, John?" Judge Chase said. "The range set by the law is six years to twenty-eight years. I give the guy ten years and everybody raises hell."

"It could be worse, I guess," Blanchard said. "You could have given him six."

"That angry editorial resulted in all those stupid letters – they don't understand what we had to go through with this case."

"What's this we stuff, Byron?" John said. "That's an old Tonto joke. But let me point out that our recommendation was the max even if I didn't expect to get it from you."

"That's exactly it. You didn't expect twenty-eight because you knew the mitigating circumstances. This was his first offense and a parent of one of the victims wanted a more merciful sentence."

"It was your decision, Judge," John concluded. "End of story."

"The problem is I don't want this one haunting me long after I've retired. I've been a fair and reasonable judge, and that's the way I want to be remembered."

"You know, Byron, I'm not exactly getting love letters myself," Blanchard said. "There are some people, even in my office, who say that I wasn't convincing enough in my first felony sentencing argument."

"You did fine, John. What I need are some people out there who give me some credit for making a Solomon-like decision. What do you think? How does this sound – Judge Byron Chase, who was credited with Solomon-like decisions during his career as a judge, announced his retirement today?"

"I'd say it sounds like you wrote it," Blanchard said, laughing.

"You know, John," Chase said, "if I presided over one more felony trial before I left, maybe I could show everyone what a hanging judge I am."

"That's not going to happen. Even if you did, you would certainly be criticized for leaning too far the other way. Don't worry about it, Judge. It'll blow over for you. As for me, I hope to try many more felony cases before I leave office."

Among those unhappy with the Walter Caine sentence was Garret Nelson, First Assistant State's Attorney. He had a nagging feeling throughout the entire proceedings that Blanchard was not taking his advice. How many times, he thought, had Blanchard begun talking during a meeting right when he was in the middle of a sentence? It was not tactful, and it was rude and unnecessary. If Blanchard had listened to his more experienced Assistant State's Attorney, the Caine case, as well as others, would have had a better result. That's when he made his decision.

"Hi, Garret, what's up?" Blanchard said as Garret entered his office.

"Need to talk to you," Garret said.

"Sure."

"Here's the thing, John," Garret began. "I've been in this office as an Assistant State's Attorney for twelve years. During that time, a few of the assistants have become Associate Judges, one became a Circuit Court Judge, and five or six have gone into private practice. I've hung in."

"I appreciate that, Garret," John Blanchard said. "You've been a lot of help."

"Well, I just don't want to help anymore; I want to be the State's Attorney. I think I have a great deal to offer."

"I think that's right. There are a hundred one counties in this state. You should be able to find one where the State's Attorney is not running for re-election or where a guy might be vulnerable because he just hasn't done the job."

"John, I live here. This is where I was born and where I grew up ... I think I've found the county where the State's Attorney is vulnerable. It's right here."

Judge Byron Chase's opinion of himself was not shared by everyone. He was sure that he had been a "fair and reasonable" judge. Those were his words to John Blanchard on the golf course. But how fair and reasonable had he been off the Bench? Don't ask Mrs. Byron Chase. What she knew about him was that he sometimes spent long evenings away from her and didn't return until early morning. She knew that she was no longer treated as his wife; that she had been told numerous times that if she didn't like his style of living, she could leave; and that she had no affection for him. No, he wasn't being seen in bars or with women of ill repute, as they used to say. He was seeing one woman, a woman who was employed right there in the courthouse. Mary Walton and Judge Chase met every Thursday night in a room at the Abraham Lincoln Hotel.

The judge wasn't very adept at foreplay, and his lovemaking was as quick and thunderous as the slamming of his gavel. However, his pillow talk was often casual and verbose. Talking about work would not be that pleasant or interesting for the typical mistress. As a listener, however, Mary Walton was one in a million. She hung on every word.

"Some people think I'm too young to retire at fifty-five," he told Mary, "but I've been through the wars. I was Chief Judge for a few years, you know, and that wasn't a walk in the park."

"But you were good at that job."

"I suppose so. I did keep things snapping around here. It wasn't particularly appreciated, though. I think some of the guys on the Bench think they have the world by the balls. They start work about nine thirty, out at three, and get paid a hundred fifty-five thou."

"I think some of them are overpaid," Mary said.

"Some of them," Chase agreed. "I get a kick out of the Mexican kid who came over from the Federal Attorney's office. He's a cracker. Ever see him do an arraignment in Spanish to some of those South American defendants? Once after he did that, he told everyone in the courtroom that he did Japanese, too. Funny guy!"

"Do you really have to retire?"

"Don't have to. Want to. I gave up a pretty good practice to become a judge, so I might think about getting involved again in the practice. Maybe I'll handle a little work for one of the better firms in town. I won't have to worry about the bucks very much. The judicial retirement deal is pretty good."

"You're not still sorry about the Walter Caine sentence, are you?" Mary asked.

"Yeah, I should have given the bastard the max, but if I did, everybody would be carping at me for being too tough on him. It's lose-lose."

"For the record, I think that you were right on target. That poor Reverend Goodwin made a lot of sense."

"Want to do it again?" asked the Honorable Byron Chase.

John Blanchard couldn't believe what he was hearing. Nelson was going to challenge him in the next election. The first thing I'm going to do after he declares is fire his ass, he thought. But then, he had a better idea. This time he met with Judge Chase in the judge's chambers.

"Judge, I would be the last man in the world," Blanchard began, "to push you into retirement, but I have another reason for asking. Have you made up your mind with certainty that you're calling it a day on the Bench?"

"As you know, I've let it be known that I was on my last voyage," said Judge Chase, who was an avid weekend sailor at the Lake Shore Club. "Don't have the sea legs anymore. It's just a matter of when we reach land. You didn't know I was an old sailor, did you?"

"So that means yes you're going to retire but you haven't decided quite when, right?"

"Aye, you've got it, mate," Chase said.

"Here's what I have in mind," Blanchard said. "I came here from Chicago to win a close election for State's Attorney. I'd like to stay here, but I've started to think about a new job."

"You want my spot on the Bench," Chase said, flatly.

"Exactly, Judge. If you were to retire before the end of your term, I think you would have enough influence to get the other Circuit Court Judges to support me to replace you. Then, of course, I could run at an advantage in the election."

"Now, why would I do that?" asked Judge Chase.

"Because I'm the best man for the job."

"No, no, that's not it," the judge said. "Give it another try."

"What do you want, Byron?" Blanchard asked.

"The Caine sentencing has done a job on me. I'm getting it from all sides. That's what's delaying my retirement announcement. I need to do something to put that out of everybody's mind. Any ideas?"

"You want me..." said a puzzled Blanchard, "You want me to figure out how you can be more popular?"

"Not popular per se, just looked at in awe. That's not asking much, is it?"

"And how do I accomplish this?"

"You're the guy who wants to sit on a Bench. Figure it out."

State's Attorney John Blanchard was not a happy man. His First Assistant State's Attorney had announced that he would be running for State's Attorney in the next election, he was still getting some heat from the public on the relatively short sentence received by Walter Caine, and now Judge Byron Chase wanted him to come up with an idea that would improve the judge's image before the judge supported him for the Bench. He took his burden to the person sitting in the closest nearby office, Mary Walton.

"Look," Blanchard said to Mary, "I see you chatting with Judge Chase once in a while. You're on pretty good terms with him, aren't you?"

Mary hadn't realized that anyone noticed her occasional public moments with the judge. "Oh, sure. He's always friendly, even when he's busy."

"Maybe you can help me," Blanchard said. "Actually, what I mean is maybe you can help him."

"Just tell me how," Mary said.

"He's concerned about his legacy as a judge now that he might retire. All that's keeping him from submitting his resignation from the Bench now is his concern about how the public viewed his decision on the Walter Caine sentencing. Have any ideas for the old bastard?"

"I guess you don't like him very much," Mary said.

"I thought that he would be more cooperative on another matter, but all he's thinking about is how good he looks to the public."

"I do have one idea," Mary said. "If you don't ask me how I know this, I'll tell you something that might help."

"Okay," Blanchard said.

"The judge's wife is a gullible religious fanatic. He wanted to give Caine a longer sentence, but it was Judge Chase's wife who was zealously influenced by Reverend Goodwin's suggestion of a ten-year sentence. She told the judge that she had a vision in her dreams that God told her that He needed Caine to be free before too long to do His work. The woman's nuts."

"That's incredible. He told you that?"

Mary thought maybe she went too far in relating this information when she heard Blanchard's reaction. "He told it to me in strict confidence. I just wondered if there was a way that we could show the judge's soft side to his advantage. Let's say that he, not his wife, was really influenced by Reverend Goodwin's statement due to the judge's religious beliefs. Then, demonstrate that he must have been guided by the hand of God, because Caine now appears to be doing some good from his prison with his published articles."

"Mary, you're as nuts as the judge's wife."

"Don't you see that leaking the information that the judge was guided by his religious beliefs through the intercession of Reverend Goodwin would give the judge an image that would be truly memorable? ... On the other hand, not everyone would like the idea that the judge is consulting God for his judicial decisions."

"The main problem," Blanchard said, "is that Chase doesn't want to appear to have been too easy on defendants. Listening to an all-merciful God will only leave a lasting impression that he wasn't tough enough."

"You're right," Mary agreed. "I guess I don't have an easy answer for you."

"How does this sound?" Blanchard asked. "What if I wrote a column in The State Journal-Register supporting the judge's decision? I will praise the judge for his decision, pointing out that he's a man who looked at all factors and made a Solomon-like decision. Yeah, that's it, a Solomon-like decision. The judge will like that. If Chase likes what I wrote, that's all I care about," the soon-to-be former State's Attorney said.

Blanchard mused about his cleverness. He was going to make the judge look good, and the judge, pleased, will resign and support Blanchard for the appointment to the Bench in his place. Those who are critical of Blanchard for not being effective enough to produce a tougher sentence will no longer matter because he'll no longer care; he'll be on his way to the Bench. That means he would no longer have to be concerned about Garret Nelson's ambitions for his job; Nelson can have it. And so it was that this column appeared the following week in the State J-R:

WHEN MERCY MAKES SENSE

George A.M. Heroux

John Blanchard*

Much has been said and argued about the recent decision by Judge Byron Chase to sentence Walter Caine to ten years in prison when he could have sentenced him to as long as twenty-eight years. My office also has been criticized for not convincing the judge that a longer sentence was warranted and necessary.

It is a judge's responsibility to consider all of the information available. That includes considering every aspect of the defendant's life prior to the crime, everything that is offered by the prosecution in aggravation, and the testimony of those who knew the defendant the best, his family and his friends. The judge must also weigh the impact of the defendant's crime on those who were affected, the families of the victims.

The victims were three young women who died as a result of the defendant's drunk driving. The father of one of the victims wanted no more than a ten-year sentence for the defendant. He demonstrated compassion and a degree of forgiveness in his recommendation. Solomon, himself, was not faced with a more difficult judicial decision.

The judge ruled with his brain, his experience, and his heart. Like Solomon, he made the right decision.

*The Honorable John Blanchard is the Sangamon County State's Attorney.

Chapter Nineteen

There was only one day of glory left for Judge Byron Chase. He had submitted his resignation, and John Blanchard had been chosen to replace him on the Bench. All that was left now was one enormous retirement party. Oddly, Mrs. Byron Chase asked to be excused. She knew with certainly a few weeks before the event that she would suffer a migraine the night of the party. St. Jonah, Protector of the Prepared, had appeared in one of her dreams to warn her. That did not prevent the judge from inviting friends and neighbors as well as everyone employed in any way in the courthouse, including Mary Walton. More surprisingly to some of those in attendance, Byron Chase arrived with Mary on his arm. He not only didn't care whether anyone knew he was having an affair with Mary, he had decided to flaunt it.

    The venue for the festivities was a private club by Springfield Lake. A dark, winding road was the entranceway to the club from the main road, which itself was a poorly lit two-lane road leading to the highway. Certainly one advantage of having his retirement party at the club was its privacy – no riff-raff here – leaving the group of mostly legal scholars and wannabees free to party without outside observation. Alcohol was plentiful.

    "Come on, Mary, let's get out of here," Chase said after a long period at the party.

    "But this is your party, Byron," the surprised Mary said.

    "I've done enough celebrating here. They'll be glad I'm gone. Are you going to come with me or not?"

"Of course, but why don't you let me drive? I haven't had so much to drink as you have."

"Ah, little Mary doesn't want to ride with a drunk driver. You have an excellent point, my dear. I am indeed drunk – and deservedly so. What you don't know is that I had a problem before I ever ascended to the mighty Bench, and I continue to have a problem. What you also don't know is that my esteemed colleagues on the Bench have been easing me off said Bench. Every one of them is sober as a judge. Funny expression, don't you think?"

"Come on, Byron, I'll take you back to my apartment. You don't want the others to see you like this."

"You are absolutely right in your impression of the situation. I should leave, but don't you agree that it is totally unfair to have those bastards thrust their holier-than-thou attitudes upon me?"

"Byron, I've never seen you like this. Please, let's go," said the alarmed Mary Walton.

"Didn't we drink together, Mary? Don't I remember having a sip or two with you in your lovely apartment?"

"Of course we did, Byron, but I've never seen you quite like this."

"Then, maybe we'd better go, Mary. Would you take me home? I'd like to go home."

"Home? Are you sure?"

The judge took one step back and slammed against the wall. "I'm going to go home and confess, Mary. I'm going to tell Mrs. Byron Chase that I've been unfaithful. I'm going to ask her to have a vision in her dreams that St. Whoever make me a Supreme Court Judge. How's that for an idea?"

Byron Chase was getting more attention than either one wanted, even though they had selected a distant area away from the bar for their conversation. One of the observers was Garret Nelson who approached them.

"Having a big night, Judge?" Garret said.

"Yes, yes, Mr. Nelson, I'm having a wonderful time, but now I should go home. The personable Ms. Walton has offered to drive me home so that I will not be your next defendant."

"Why don't I drive you, Byron? As you might remember, I don't drink. Maybe Mary would like to stay and enjoy what's left of the party."

"Hear that, Mary?" Byron said. "There's a man of integrity. He sizes up a situation and takes action. He wants to save your reputation and my life, all in one swell foop."

"Thank you, Garret," Mary said. "If you don't mind, I think I will let you drive him home."

Garret Nelson was, by far, the most athletic of the Assistant State's Attorneys. He ran track in high school and college and once broke four minutes in the mile, an accomplishment that would have been extraordinary fifty years ago but was now almost commonplace. After college, he became a marathon man. He competed in Chicago and New York and then reached the pinnacle by running the Boston marathon. He finished every race with excellent times for a thirty-eight year old but, of course, was never in the winner's circle.

Frequently over the past several years, he had thought about another kind of running, pursuing an attractive woman about his age who worked in his office. Most amazing was that both were unmarried. Naturally, it came as a surprise, then, when Garret saw Byron Chase treating her so intimately at the retirement party. He didn't like it, even though he had made no advances toward her in the time that he knew her. He decided that that mistake should be remedied as soon as possible. Imagine his surprise, however, when Mary approached him first with a suggestion that they meet after work for a cup of coffee.

"I wanted to talk to you about the other night at the Springfield Lake Club," Mary began.

"Should I have butted out?" Garret asked.

"No, I appreciated your intervention. I felt that I owed you an explanation."

"That's not the case, Mary. You don't need to tell me anything."

"I know I don't need to, but I guess I would like to. I always thought that someday you might notice me and that we could become friends."

"Truthfully," Garret said, "I would like nothing better. You have always been friendly but very formal. I thought that you didn't like me particularly."

"That's the farthest thing from the truth. Now, I just have to tell someone what's been going on. May I cry on your shoulder?"

"I would be happy to help in any way I can, Mary," Garret said, meaning it.

"The man is seventeen years older than I am, but he always treated me as though I were somebody important. I had an immature crush on him from the beginning. When he started paying all that attention to me, I was taken back at first."

"But you enjoyed it," interrupted Garret.

"Yes, I did. I had recently moved to Springfield from Peoria. I didn't mention this to anyone because I didn't want to talk about it, but I had been married. My former husband was a guy who cared more about the gambling boats than about me. He's five years younger than I am, but he acted even younger. I think his mental age was about nineteen. I suppose that's why I was fascinated by an older man giving me all that attention."

"That is quite a change," observed Garret. "Did you file for a divorce because you had enough of his gambling?"

"No, I filed for a divorce because he left me. He simply disappeared. I have no idea if he's even alive. I filed for divorce claiming desertion, then I left town and didn't leave a forwarding address. I took my maiden name back. I was Mary Butler."

"Mary, you're confiding in me, so I'm going to ask you two questions: One, should I assume that you are having an affair with Byron, and two, are you going to get out of it?"

"Yes, I have opened myself up to you, so I don't mind that you know. It was a school girl crush that got out of hand. I feel …

demeaned. And yes, I'm going to tell him that it's over. He needs to work on his marriage, not me."

"Good for you," Garret said. "Let's have another cup of coffee when you've accomplished that in no uncertain terms. I think it's time that you and I get to know each other better."

Former Judge Byron Chase had determined that he was going to "jump ship" from the relationship that he had somehow acquired with Mary Walton. The mystery was how he had accomplished that in the first place. He assumed, correctly, that she had looked up to him and, because of this, he was able to take advantage of her. Now, he would put all of that behind him, particularly since he sensed that Mary had closed the door at the retirement party. Since he had been so successful in his efforts with Mary, why could he not exercise some influence over his own wife? She needed to get back into the real world, he thought.

Are we absolutely certain that Mrs. Byron Chase was not in the real world already? Sure, her life was centered in the church, and sometimes the intensity of her religious fervor appeared peculiar to the casual observer, but who's to say that she wasn't exactly on target. After all, no one has ever returned from the dead to report the world on the other side of life. Nevertheless, Chase assumed that his view of the real world was the accurate one, so he took on the challenge of exercising his will over hers.

"I would like to have a serious talk with you," he said to her.

"All of a sudden, you want to talk to me," Mrs. Bryon Chase said.

"It is my belief that we can have a normal married relationship if we both are willing to make some changes," Chase said.

"I believe you, Byron," she said, "but you and only you need to change – no more acting like a mini-God, no more philandering, and no more ignoring me. Can you do that?"

"Yes, I will make a vow to you here and now that I will do that, but I do need changes from you."

"What do you want from me," she said, "lose weight, iron your shirts, make dinner at home more often – what?"

"No, what I have in mind is less extraordinary. ... How about letting up on this fanaticism? There, I've said it. That's what I'd like."

"You really do want to spend eternity in hell," his wife said.

"Look," a frustrated Chase said, "would you, could you consider the possibility there is no hell?"

"It's all in the Bible, Byron. You need to read that book now that you don't have to read law books."

"I appreciate the fact," Chase said, "that you believe in heaven and have dedicated your life to getting there. What you don't seem to understand is that we are all individually responsible for our after-life destinies. Don't try to control mine, and we can have a much more relaxed life now."

Apparently, Chase was unsuccessful in his attempt to dissuade Mrs. Byron Chase from her religious zeal. That night, St. Joseph, Patron of Widows, appeared with a message that Byron Chase would soon know what it was like on the other side.

Chapter Twenty

The Goodwins and the Oswalds, through the loss of Patti and Maris, became fast friends. Over the next few years, they visited each other frequently. Since the Goodwins no longer had a daughter, they were fascinated by the abundance of Oswald offspring, all daughters. They were especially intrigued with the two youngest, Marsha and Madeline, those daughters who wanted no part of the settlement money from the crash, at least not now in their idealistic age. Bill Goodwin, unfortunately, continued to deteriorate from his Parkinson's, but he had the will to live of a Job. This was encouraged and assisted by the strong and supportive Mary Goodwin. Not having expended any of the settlement money on their own luxuries, this visit took place at the still simple home of the Oswalds.

"Your home is lovely," Mary Goodwin said, thereby complimenting them for their decision not to splurge the settlement money by enhancing their residence.

"Henry has done quite well as a CPA," Jessica said. "This is a nice neighborhood with pleasant neighbors. We have no desire to change our standard of living."

"And you're still active in your work?" Bill Goodwin asked, although he already knew the answer.

"Very much so," replied Henry Oswald. "Oddly enough, all of the publicity over the tragic losses of our daughters has resulted in many more clients. I dislike admitting to such a consideration, but it seems to be true."

"I understand completely," Bill said. "As a matter of fact, I was asked to resume participation in my calling, albeit at a necessarily limited degree for an obvious reason."

"It appears that the girls have touched our lives in an unusual way long after they are no longer with us," Bill said.

"You have heard about the Fergusons, I take it," Mary said.

"Isn't that wonderful news?" Jessica said. "I suppose that's a gift in a way from their daughter, Cayla."

"How are your girls doing?" asked Mary.

"I couldn't be more pleased," Jessica said. "Of course, they will always miss Maris. She related so well to both her younger and her older sisters. Oh, sure, she had spats with the older girls about shoes and clothes, but she was always supportive when it came to anyone outside of the family. The younger girls looked up to Maris. All of that is gone now, but everyone is taking a turn replacing Maris' contributions, I think."

Neither couple mentioned Paul Sanford and his problems, although his travails were well known to both.

Cured? We'll see. Paul Sanford was a banker by profession. His expertise was in bank investments, so it was not unexpected that Paul would offer to provide Heather with some advice in the handling of her settlement funds. In the beginning, the funds were safely ensconced in certificates of deposit. Paul thought that he could do better.

"Heather," Sanford said, "As I think you know, I'm responsible for making decisions involving millions of dollars for the bank. If you want, I can help you find investments for your funds that are highly profitable while being totally secure. That's the perfect recipe for investments, to have your money grow with very little risk of loss."

"I don't know, Dad," Heather responded. "You know best. I just want to be sure that I'm covered for school and any unexpected medical expenses that might be necessary if I have repercussions from the crash. Of course, I'd like to have money to help the rest of the family also, if anyone needs it."

"I understand, Honey," Sanford said, "but in today's economy, you have to make good use of the money you have through wise investments."

There's always someone who feels that he or she knows more about investments than most everyone else. That was Sanford, although he had very little to show for his own prior efforts in the market. Heather was well aware that she could invest in certificates of deposit, money market deposit accounts, and money market funds with very little risk. But Sanford's eyes widened with the possibility of purchasing stocks, bonds, mutual funds, and real estate. These were the potentials for big payoffs, and these were the kinds of investments he foresaw as profitable for Heather – and for him. Heck, he was pretty good at picking the ponies; maybe the racetrack wouldn't be a bad idea.

"You do whatever you think is best," Heather said. "There are some CDs that are maturing. Why don't you do what you think is right with that money?"

Margaret Oswald graduated Magna Cum Laude from Southern Illinois University and now, thanks to money inherited from the estate of her sister, Maris, she was on her way to medical school. A week's vacation was desired, however, before she started school. Consequently, she decided to spend a week with an old friend who had moved to Cleveland. While there, she thought that she would look in on the one Howard Christian College student who survived the crash, Heather Sanford. Heather was delighted to see her.

"It means so much to me that you and your family care about me," Heather said. "You know I haven't seen any of the families. I just couldn't bring myself to attend any of the trial proceedings."

"I understand," Margaret said. "We lost a wonderful sister and you lost some good friends. In addition to that, I know that you were terribly injured. I hoped that I would find you recovered."

"I'm doing pretty well," Heather said. "I'll be graduating from Howard in January."

"You look great," Margaret said.

"So," Heather said, "you're on your way to medical school. That's wonderful. Maris would have been proud of you."

"Actually, the cost of medical school might have been out of reach unless I had gone way into debt as many medical students do. I don't like to think of how I've benefited from Maris' death, but that's exactly what happened. My family each received a share of the crash settlement inherited from Maris through her estate."

"Technically," Heather said, "I own the entire amount allocated to me in the settlement. My father is going to make some investments for me to make sure that the fund grows … Maybe I should consider medical school, too."

Margaret had heard rumors about Paul Sanford's problems, so she was surprised that he was involved in handling Heather's money. "This is none of my business, Heather, but do you want to entrust your money to a member of the family? I don't mean to insult you or your father."

"Thank you for saying what you think," Heather said. "To tell you the truth, I have some concerns. You know that we have had some problems in the family, don't you?"

"Yes, I've heard only because my parents were concerned about you. You know, three families have lost someone, but, thank God, you survived. We want the best for you. In a way, you're our representative now on earth whether you want to be or not."

"I hadn't thought about it that way," Heather said. "I'm so pleased that you visited and said those things. I haven't been looking at it that way at all. You see, my doctor told me that I might experience what is called survivor guilt, wondering why I wasn't killed also in that awful crash."

"Heather," Margaret assured her, "we are all pleased that you lived. Never doubt that."

"Your parents have been very considerate. I don't know if you know it, but your mother has sent me letters of encouragement all along."

"That doesn't surprise me at all," Margaret said. "I happen to have a great father also. He and my mother have told us that they're not going to use any part of their inherited share just in case my sisters or I need some money in the future."

"Do you mind if I ask you a question about the money your parents have from the settlement?" Heather asked.

"No, what would you like to know?"

Heather was clearly concerned about the wisdom of having her father manage her funds. "Have they invested the money somehow to make more money? That's what my father says we need to do."

"You know," Margaret said, "my father is a CPA. He wants only the best for us, and he cares about you, also. What would you think about his reviewing investments before your father makes them? We can do it in a way that your father will never know. Just tell him you would like to review any investment before it happens so that you learn. Then, fax the info to me and I'll pass it on to my father. What do you think? Admittedly, I'm encouraging a little deception here, but it would be better to be safe than sorry."

Knowing what we know about Paul Sanford's character, it is not astonishing that Henry Oswald discovered that Sanford's proposed investments were earmarked, through devious means, for Sanford's savings account. Heather was quick to abort this misuse of her money.

"What do you mean you don't want me to handle your investments," Sanford said, virtually exploding.

"I'm sorry," Heather said, "but I've decided to stay with low interest, safe investments."

"Do you know what the hell you're talking about?" screamed Sanford.

"Please, Dad, you're frightening me," Heather said, with alarm.

"You're just like your damn mother," Sanford said. "You don't want me to succeed. You don't want me to get my reputation back. You want me to suffer. Your mother put you up to this, didn't she?"

"Mom had nothing to do with it. I've made up my mind all by myself."

"Well, if it wasn't your mother it was your sisters. Elaine has always hated me. Both of you accused me of something I never did. You owe me for that."

"I'm sorry about that. Maybe we were wrong. We're not really sure. Anyway, Elaine and Carrie had nothing to do with my decision either."

Sanford lost all that he may have learned in anger control sessions. "I have a Power of Attorney here that my lawyer prepared. I want you to sign it ... now! This document will let you concentrate on your studies and on getting well again. I'm really tired of being the scapegoat for everything that goes wrong here. I'm still your father. You need to listen to me about the money."

"I can't do that," Heather said, standing up to her father.

Sanford turned and slammed the wall with his fist, drawing blood on his knuckles. "I warn you," he said, "if you don't sign this, I'm going to make life miserable for you, your mother, and your sisters. Do you understand?"

"I'll sign it," Heather said, "on one condition, that you stay out of our lives forever except to give me the money when I need it for school or if Mom or my sisters need some money. Will you do that?"

"Yes, yes. Just sign it."

Heather scrawled along the signature line of the Power of Attorney, put it back into the envelope, and handed it to Sanford. Without a thank you or a goodbye, he rushed out the door. A short time later, he looked at the document. Along the signature line, Heather had written "Heather refuses."

Chapter Twenty-One

There was a great deal of interest in Walter Caine's growing number of articles. The Time Magazine article initiated considerable discussion in legal circles, among prison administrators, throughout the justice system, and in public circles. Although his observations and comments made indisputable sense, many wondered why he was allowed to make them from a prison setting. Had Warden Gary Watkins lost control? Had the prison system gone soft? Nevertheless the columns and articles continued. Virtually every one of the pieces written by him was thoroughly researched and expressed information and opinions that instigated some action by courts, prosecutors, or law enforcement.

He was allowed to spend so much time in research and in writing that the warden provided another prisoner to assist him in the library. This new helper was a man about half a dozen years older than Walter and was serving time for armed robbery, apparently made necessary in his mind to provide funds for his relentless desire to gamble. When he arrived at the library, he introduced himself as Billy Butler.

"What's with all this work you do?" Billy asked.

"I don't want to just put in time," Walter said. "Being busy is going to make my eight and a half years go by a whole lot faster."

"So you're really in with the warden, huh?" Butler said.

"He believes I'm doing some good. So far, it seems to be working."

"Now that I have this plush job, I'll warn you that you're not all that popular in the trenches."

"What do you mean?" Walter asked.

"The word is out that you're getting special privileges because you have people reading what you write. Is that right?"

"I still eat the same food and sleep in the same kind of cell as everyone else here," Walter stated.

"Okay, I have no problem with what you're doing. Tell me something. How do you know where the articles are going to be published?" Butler asked.

"Now, all the articles are being printed in the same newspaper, The Chicago Tribune. The warden arranged for me to write a weekly column, so they all go to the same newspaper," Walter explained.

"That's what some of the inmates heard. That's why I'm here. A few strings were pulled to get me this job so I can give you a message," Butler said.

"What are you talking about?"

"There are some rackets being run outside by guys in this prison. The general, the godfather, the boss, whatever you want to call him, is serving time right here."

"What does that have to do with me?" Caine asked.

"You are going to issue some orders through your columns. You have no choice in this. If you don't cooperate, you're a dead man. There is absolutely no doubt about that. Remember a tall, dark guy with never-ending eyebrows, a mean-looking hombre? He was hassling you when you first arrived."

"Sure," Walter said, "prisoner No. 5416."

"You got it. One word from him and some very bad things would happen to you. He wouldn't just kill you. There would be a series of accidents. You'd lose a hand, maybe, or your tongue would disappear. I would recommend total cooperation."

"I can't just change my columns to contain messages."

"You don't have to change the meaning of the columns. All you have to do is insert some words in a specific place in the second and fourth paragraphs of every article. You're a smart guy. You can do that and still say whatever you want to say."

"Wonderful," Walter said. "I get to do a puzzle every week."

"You got something better to do with your time?" Butler asked. "Going to any ballgames?"

"I guess I could do that. I mean, it would be possible for me to do that, but it doesn't fit with my plans. I don't want to break the law again. I don't want to cause any more misery."

"There's nothing, nothing, you can do but cooperate," Butler said. "None of this is my idea. They picked me out of the crowd to get into the library. I didn't have a chance, either. If we don't do what they want, they come after both of us."

"All right," Walter said. "I'll do it but only until I figure how to stop cooperating without either of us getting maimed."

Warden Gary Watkins was pleased with his prolific prisoner. The challenge was to maintain a balance between lauding Caine for writing the columns and seeing to it that his prison time was punishment, nevertheless, for the felony he committed. There remained some cynicism within and without the criminal justice conglomerate. Many were impressed with the quality and quantity of Walter's writing. Others were of the opinion that Walter was playing the warden and the Corrections Department. Indeed, Walter was sincere in his attitude to save lives by encouraging safe driving practices and discouraging impaired and distracted driving. He documented every column with studious research and opinions based on his own catastrophic experience.

"I'm intrigued," Gary Watkins said, "with how you have managed to find new slants, new ideas week after week."

"Having access to the legal search tools helps a whole lot," Walter said.

"You're the first person, of course, to use the legal research capability in this way. We know that we have any number of jailhouse lawyers, prisoners looking for loopholes and writing appeals."

"My long-range plan," Walter explained, "is to report consequences of impaired driving by writing about real cases, so readers understand that I'm not describing video games or non-fiction. I think that I can personalize these tragedies so that there is a real image of the losses that have occurred. I'll report on numbers, too, so everyone can fully appreciate the extent of the problem."

"I think that will be effective," Watkins said. "Any other ideas?"

"Sure. I'd like to aim some columns at underage drinkers, make them understand that it has been proven time and time again that alcohol has an adverse effect on the development of the brain. We all want to be as smart as we can. I want to explain that drinking will only help them to dumb down, not get smarter."

"Okay, keep them coming here to my office. If I approve the columns, out they'll go to the Trib."

"There's something else that you need to know," Walter said.

"Yes?"

"I have a problem," Walter announced abruptly.

"What sort of problem?" Watkins asked.

Prisoner No. 5416, known simply as Bull, was animalistic in nature, but he was far from stupid. He was a gang member and leader by the time he was fourteen. Drugs, prostitution, illegal gambling, shakedowns – these were all part of his modus operandi. The FBI eventually got him for income tax evasion, a charge that has put underworld characters in prison since the Twenties. A judge, who may or may not have been on the payroll, as rumored, sentenced him to eighteen months of day for day time. Clearly, this would not put a chink in his continuing criminal career or his racketeering leadership. Now, he had developed a clever method of issuing orders to his henchmen through the circulation of Walter Caine's newspaper column.

"Here are the words for the week, Walter," Butler said. "Bull said to tell you that you're doing a great job."

"I could care less what Bull thinks," Caine said. "I'm dealing with self-preservation. That's it!"

"I know it, you know it, he knows it," Butler said. "Anyway, here they are: Second, man, go, and Vegas.

"Not exactly an unbreakable code," Walter said. "He's sending his second in command to Las Vegas."

"Yeah, probably," Butler said.

Walter began writing his column for the week. It was a report on new legislation prohibiting text messaging while driving and cell phone use in construction and school zones, along with his analysis of the possible difficulties in enforcing the new laws. In the second paragraph, he noted that this was the second time in two years that the Legislature, to a man and woman, indicated a desire to take action on these problems. In the fourth paragraph, he commented that the police would probably go easy on enforcement in the beginning to give the public an opportunity to be fully aware of the laws. Nevertheless, he advised the public not to gamble on how severely the laws would be enforced. That would be as risky as a trip to a St. Louis gambling boat.

Yes, he changed Vegas to St. Louis in the list provided by Bull. Three columns later, Bull's men were utterly confused. It was the policy of the warden not to provide the Trib to prisoners. The Sun Times was the newspaper of choice of the inmates. Consequently, it was four weeks into Bull's grand communications plan that he discovered Walter's bold move.

Nobody crosses Bull, he thought; he took immediate action. He was so angry at Walter's failure to follow his exact orders that he determined that he would handle this "traitor" himself. His weapon of choice was a rusty piece of pipe that had been shaped to a fine point in the shop by fellow prisoners adept at such refinements. He had no intention of killing Walter, but he did want to cause considerable pain, even if he was caught doing it. Everyone had to know that you don't mess with Bull.

Bull's request to visit the library was approved for the stated reason that he needed to do some additional research on the legitimacy of tax evasion charges against a man who had no documented evidence of income. Watkins had expected this visit, of course. Well positioned in the library was one of his most capable guards, a man who eerily looked and acted like Arnold Schwarzenegger. When Bull made his move, Watkins' Schwarzenegger made his. In seconds, Bull found himself prostrate with his arm twisted behind him, held fast by the big guard. Then, something happened that the warden did not foresee.

A second prisoner, idly flipping through magazines, struck the unsuspecting guard with lightening speed, a thrust to the back with a weapon very similar to the one Bull had in his possession. That weapon was now still held loosely in the hand that was pinned behind Bull.

"Look out!" screamed Walter, but it was much too late. Bull shook off the Schwarzenegger look-a-like who was now in a puddle of blood and moved rapidly toward a terrified Walter Caine. Bull's protector closed and blocked the entrance to the library. Bull never reached his target. With remarkable agility and accuracy, Butler landed a steel chair directly across Bull's calves, sending him sprawling. With a second blow from Butler and the chair, Bull dropped his weapon and fought off unconsciousness. Butler picked up the dropped weapon and drove it into Bull's neck. Bull's comrade dropped his weapon and put his hands in the air as guards burst through the door.

"God, Billy, you saved my life," Walter exclaimed.

"I brought you the problem, Buddy. I wasn't about to let it end this way," Butler said.

This particular day in the lives of Walter Caine and Billy Butler would have significant input on the day that both were eligible for parole.

Totally unaware of their son's brush with death or serious injury, Ed and Betty Caine had other concerns. Johnny's visits with them grew longer and longer. That was just fine with the Caines, but it made them suspicious of his mother's concern for him. This prompted Ed to do something unusual. Even though he had no idea how to go about it, he eventually located and hired a private detective to look into Debby's care of Johnny. He discovered in a very short time that Debby often left Johnny alone late into the night while she and her new husband partied elsewhere. When he documented that Debby and her husband were drinking in excess and using drugs, the Caines petitioned the court for sole custody of Johnny.

"You have no right to do this," Debby shouted into the phone.

"We have every right as Johnny's grandparents," Ed responded. "You are an unfit mother and we intend to have Johnny stay with us full-time."

"The court will never allow that," she said. "Your son is a jailbird."

Ed was patient. "We'll see, then, Debby, how the court responds to our evidence on camera of your drinking excessively and using cocaine. We have that evidence now. We're ready to go to court.

"You're a sneaky old bastard, aren't you?" Debby said.

"Yes, I am," Ed answered, "but I have right on my side."

"Take him. I really don't give a rat's ass. I'm tired of catering to the kid and being responsible for him. I won't fight the petition. He's all yours."

Chapter Twenty-Two

It's paradoxical, is it not, that many not-for-profit organizations begin with such idealistic goals but then find themselves overcome by the desire to raise money? It's a never-ending cycle: somehow obtain seed money, perform services, pay personnel to add more services, pay personnel to raise more and more money to add more services, hire better paid personnel mostly to raise money to pay for those personnel, reduce services, raise more money to reinstate services, hire more fund raisers to pay for that and to pay for the new fundraisers. Whew! That pretty much described, in rather haphazard terms, Americans Against Intoxicated Drivers.

The single- and simple-minded Jack Northrup, Executive Director of AAID, thought that the solution for financial woes was not to cut staff or salaries but to raise money. His immediate targets were the recipients of the settlement from the Springfield DUI crash that took the lives of three Howard Christian students and severely injured a fourth. His approach was obtrusive at best.

"Mrs. Goodwin," he said into the phone, "this is Jack Northrup, the Executive Director of AAID in Dallas. I believe that our organization provided some assistance to your family in that terrible tragedy that took your daughter's life."

"Yes, I remember someone from your local chapter sitting with me during the sentencing. I'm sorry I don't remember her name."

"I understand that you received a financial settlement from the civil action," Northrup said. "That's correct, isn't it?"

"Well, yes we did," Mary said. "I suppose it's all right to tell you that."

"I don't know how much you know about our organization, but we've assisted many victims of drunk driving crashes, and we try to educate the public to prevent future such tragedies."

"Yes, I understand that AAID does that," Mary said, wondering why on earth the Executive Director of this well-known organization was calling her.

"I thought that you might want to help us with our financial situation. We haven't asked victims in the past for help, but we need to raise funds quickly to continue to help victims. Do you think that you can help?"

Mary was a bit surprised at the request. After all, money from a civil case is not a windfall. Litigation awards are simply to compensate victims for losses, in this case the loss of Patti's future income and love and affection lost to the family plus, of course, funeral expenses and any other bills submitted to them in connection with the crash. "What kind of contribution were you looking for?" Mary asked.

"We could really use a major donation because of rising costs in serving the needs of victims through an increased staff, especially in our national office," the AAID Executive Director said.

"I'm not sure what we could do. My husband is in rather poor health. We may face some unforeseen expenses."

"What if I call you back again this time tomorrow?" he said. "Perhaps you can think in terms of several hundred thousand or even a hundred thousand. I'll call you back tomorrow."

Well, that went pretty well, thought Northrup. If this works just once, it will take care of my salary for six months. Then he moved on to a phone call to the Oswalds. Jessica answered the phone. He gave her pretty much the same spiel. Always pleasant, Jessica almost gave him an affirmative answer until he mentioned the several hundred thousand dollar figure. The call ended by Northrup saying that he would call her tomorrow also. The third call was answered by the now-retired CEO, Danielle Ferguson.

"You want me to do what?" she said.

"We have a dire need here, Mrs. Ferguson," Northrup said. "Our request would represent only a small portion of the settlement you received."

"We'll consider a contribution, perhaps, but we would have to make the decision on the amount, if any, based on your use of the money. Please send me a copy of your last audited P&L and balance sheet along with a five-year plan specifying goals and objectives for your company."

"Ahh, I would have to get permission from my board to provide you with financial statements. Our plan for the future is really a three-year plan, and it involves reorganization of state and local chapters to reflect a leaner, meaner machine."

"I'll await those documents, then," Danielle said.

Jack Northrup was not so upbeat after that call, but he had one call more. The AAID staff research to find telephone numbers was not very effective. In the next instance, the number was Paul Sanford's cell phone. Halleluiah!

"Are you kidding me?" Sanford said. "Heather's not about to part with any of that money. I'd have to have a heart attack for her to send any of it my way. Send you guys some money? Forget it!"

The cocky, confident Northrup correctly concluded that getting money from victims who were awarded compensatory damages in civil suits would be more difficult than he thought.

The following morning, his phone rang. The caller was Tom Lansing.

"Mr. Northrup, I understand that you have been contacting my clients to solicit donations from our settlement," Tom said.

"Well, yes, that's true," Northrup admitted. "We did provide some services. I wanted to give them the opportunity to make a contribution toward our efforts."

"Not my idea of class," Tom said. "You provided the services free, did you not? You told them that services were free before you provided those services, isn't that true?"

"Yes, that's true, and I want to make it clear that we are not charging now. We simply asked for financial participation in our efforts."

"What is your salary, Mr. Northrup?"

"I don't think that's the issue here," Northrup responded.

"I believe it's very much so the issue. A few of the families have asked me for advice on this matter. Unless I can get some information on how funds are used, including a detailed report on salaries paid to staff and what they do for these salaries, I will certainly recommend that they make no contributions to AAID."

"Don't you understand that we were very helpful to these people in a very difficult time? I believe that they owe us, that they should be anxious to assist us in our time of need."

Tom was now very firm in his response: "For now, it will be my advice to the families to contribute nothing. If you want to send me the information I requested, I'll review the documents and then determine if I want to change my advice."

"You're difficult at best, Mr. Lansing," Northrup said.

"Yes," Tom said flatly.

"All right," Northrup said, "I'll send you what I can. In the meantime, it occurs to me that your fee for handling the case for all of the families must have been huge. Would you consider making a donation from that fee?"

Don Dolittle lived up to his name most of the time. That's not entirely fair. There really wasn't that much to do. He was AAID's computer expert. He set up a number of unique programs and then simply waited for problems to occur. For the most part, there were no problems, but he was always on hand just in case. Originally, he worked for the Florida state chapter. He came to Northrup's attention after he set up programs in Florida that provided very personal financial information about every victim that received any assistance from AAID and about everyone who ever made a contribution to AAID, regardless of how large or small.

"How are we doing with compiling information about victims' families who collected big judgment awards in civil actions?" Northrup asked.

"We have the state execs making phone calls," Dolittle responded, "then the info will be fed into a computer program I wrote. It's a long project, might take, oh, six months."

"The sooner the better," Northrup said. "That's going to be one valuable list. You know, it occurs to me that after we contact these people, we could sell the list to other organizations that raise money. We could get a pretty good price for the list, couldn't we?"

"Not a doubt," Dolittle answered. "There are mailing list companies. They would act as our agents so we wouldn't have to do the marketing."

"It would look better, also, if we weren't directly involved."

"Jack, do you want me to put together a report for the Board of Directors on what we're doing to raise money from victim families?"

"Are you kidding me?" Northrup said. "They're all victims and victim family members. I'm sure we'd get some flack. I've run three not-for-profits, and I've always had one important guiding principle to my style of management."

"What's that, Jack?"

"I do whatever I think is best, then I let the Board know what I'm doing. That avoids obstructionism, stilted thinking, and bleeding hearts."

"Jack, you're brilliant," Dolittle kissed up.

Chapter Twenty-Three

Remember Harry Foster of Foster Ford? The company's insurance premium took quite a bump after the settlement, and the company had a slimmer profit margin after paying out a million dollars, but it not only survived but prospered in the aftermath, thanks to Ford Manufacturing Company outdoing the competition in profitability while the other manufacturers were traveling to Washington, D.C. for bailout money. Foster did away with the company's policies that allowed the funding of quota parties and let employees use company cars for personal use. Harry, himself, however, enjoyed cocktails occasionally at that very same Springfield club that hosted Judge Byron Chase's retirement party. Harry was sitting quietly, enjoying his drinks - yes, a number of them – when he noticed a familiar figure at the bar.

"Byron, is that you?" Harry asked.

"Harry, how are you?" Byron responded. "You've decided to come out into the world."

"Sure," Harry responded. "I can't stay in hiding forever. Besides, they only took me for a million. Easy come, easy go."

Byron Chase approached Harry's table and sat down. "Want some company?"

"Sure, Byron. It's a privilege to be in the presence of a former judge. How's life off the Bench?"

"Strange. My wife hasn't quite figured out how to put me back in her life. She prays about it a good deal. I'm even considering going to church with her, but I haven't made any rash promises yet."

"Wouldn't hurt you a bit," Harry said. "Even some of my employees have been going to church since they all got shook up by that accident."

"I put that guy away," Byron said. "Remember?"

"Sure, I was at the sentencing. What you did was very merciful, Byron. I know that you could have sent him to prison for a long, long time. I understand that he's about a third of the way home."

"I guess that's right," Byron said. "It's been almost three years since he was sentenced. Another five and a half and he'll be back in society and trying to get his license back."

"Not everybody liked your sentence, I understand," Harry said.

"Nah. You can't please everyone no matter what you do," Byron responded.

"I'll drink to that, Byron," Harry said, lifting his glass.

Harry and Byron were kindred souls. Quite a few more glasses were lifted in the next few hours. Finally, Byron decided to call it a night. "I'm out of here, Harry. It's been a blast. Maybe I'll go home and pray with my wife."

"Byron, I doubt that you know how, but I'd recommend giving it a shot."

Byron sat in his car for a few minutes trying to decide whether he could make it home after drinking. He decided that if he drove slowly and very deliberately, he could make the short trip home. Of course, that's always what inebriated drivers think. Unfortunately, often they are mistaken. He began his way cautiously down the winding road that led out of the club's property. Just over a rise in the road, he heard an unusual sound coming from under the hood of his car. He pulled over to the side of the road. Steam was coming from underneath the hood, and a warning light indicated that the engine was hot. The motor went quiet.

"What the hell!" he said to himself and everything around him. "God damn it."

He reached for his cell phone. Dead. No response. "Christ, I forgot to charge it."

Deeply frustrated, he sat quietly for a few minutes, wondering if he might just sleep in the car. Maybe he'd be sober when he awoke in a few hours. It doesn't work that way exactly. Alcohol metabolizes in the blood at about a drink an hour, so that short-term sleeping, coffee, or food won't help that much; only time will rid the body of alcohol.

Damn, he thought, I guess I'll just have to walk back to the club and call a cab. It's probably a mile back. I'll get someone to check the car in the morning. Left with no other viable plan, Byron stepped out of the car and began walking along the side of the road back toward the club.

Harry decided to stay a bit longer but not much longer. He had no wife to accompany in prayer or anything else. It had been about a dozen years since his divorce from a woman who had no interest in any of Harry's interests. She was interested in spending Harry's money, however, although she thought that he could make much more of it if he just put his mind to it. She had an odd assortment of friends from bridge players to tennis players to theatre performers. In general, she was good at spending money that Harry earned without ever giving Harry any credit for his efforts. She was happiest when she was not home. It came as no surprise to Harry, then, when she announced that she wanted a divorce. She called it mental cruelty because Harry didn't pay enough attention to her. In reality, she had met a wealthier man. She married him five days after her divorce from Harry was final.

Occasionally, Harry felt sorry for himself as he was doing the night he ran into Byron Chase at the club. He, too, wondered if he should be driving after consuming alcohol for a period of about three hours, but he, too, decided that he could drive slowly and carefully without any problem.

The dark, winding road with a slight rise proved to be unfortunate for both Harry and the former judge. Harry saw Byron Chase only after he was immediately in front of him. He could not react in time to brake or turn the car away. There are excellent reasons for drunk driving laws. A drunk driver can not perceive depth or proximity of surroundings, is not able to react quickly, and has very little control of manual skills.

As forecast by St. Joseph in Mrs. Byron Chase's dream, Byron's wife became a widow that night.

When Sergeant Kirk Olden, a man trained in notification procedures, gave the bad news to Mrs. Byron Chase, he was shocked to hear that she not only knew that her husband was dead but she knew how he died. Was she really communicating with saints in her dreams to the extent that she actually saw the future or were her fanatical beliefs such that she convinced herself that what she experienced in dreams was real?

Our knowledge of unknown powers beyond the ordinary is still severely limited. People pray and expect answers that reflect their wishes. Others pray and accept the responses they receive as what is meant to be, even if the response does not fulfill the requests. Then, of course, there is the power of believing that has been demonstrated throughout the centuries from idol worship to self-immolation to mass murders, all in a sincere belief that it is God's will. Fortunately for all of us, most of us have simple but genuine creeds while hoping for the best on the other side.

"I'm sorry," Sergeant Olden said. "This news must be very traumatic for you to hear. Perhaps you heard a news report that there was a death near the club. Sometimes they do that but don't identify the person until next of kin are notified."

"Yes, I did hear that on WTAX. Thank you for coming and confirming my worst fears."

Sergeant Olden hesitated, wondering what else he could possibly say. "You'll be hearing from the coroner's office. Are you all right?"

"Yes, I'm quite used to his not being with me, except this time, of course, he won't be returning."

"Is there anyone I can call for you?" Sergeant Olden asked.

"No, no, thank you, Sergeant," Mrs. Byron Chase said. "I think I'll go pray now for Byron's soul. Tomorrow, I'll make arrangements with the church. He wasn't a very religious man, but the priest will honor him with a Mass anyway, I'm sure."

State's Attorney Garret Nelson had just returned from a dinner date with the woman who was now his fiancé, Mary Walton. During dinner, they had discussed wedding plans. Mary was truly happy. The last few years had been magical for her. The short relationship that she had with Byron Chase was long forgotten. Even the reason for getting involved with the judge was no longer a matter of any concern, a simple blip on her ancient radar screen. Garret was looking forward to a good night's sleep; he would be in court most of the day tomorrow on an armed robbery case. He didn't sleep long.

As the sun rose, his phone rang. State Police Sergeant Kirk Olden was on the phone. "I thought that you might want to know about an arrest I made last night for a DUI death and especially the name of the victim."

Of course, Garret was shocked to hear that the former judge had been killed in a freak occurrence. A day later, Harry Foster was charged with DUI; that was all for the time being. There would be an exhaustive investigation. State's Attorney Nelson had to determine whether Foster's impairment was responsible for Byron Chase's death.

The following morning, Garret wasn't surprised to get a phone call from Norman Caswell asking for an appointment.

"I'll be representing Harry Foster regardless of what the charges are," Norman said. "My hope is that the charge will be DUI and only DUI. Can we talk about it?"

"I'll have to see a completed investigation report before I make any decision," Garret said.

"This is a preemptive strike, I guess," Norman said. "As you know, Harry Foster is a successful businessman and an important community leader. His business took a real blow as a result of the Howard Christian College students' crash. As you remember, I represented his employee in the case. If we can avoid a prolonged period of indecision on this, it would be helpful."

"There won't be a prolonged period of indecision in this office, Norm," Garret said. "When I have all the facts, I'll make a decision."

"This was an accident, Garret, no more than that. As you well know, there is no presumption of criminal recklessness just because a driver is intoxicated. You have to prove that the cause of the death was his impaired driving. Byron was walking alongside a dark road at the bottom of a crest in the hill. There's no way that anyone who was cold sober could have avoided hitting him."

"There's no point in discussing the merits of the defense right now, Norman. I've been a prosecutor for almost a few decades. I happen to believe that the presumption we used to have made sense. I believe that a sober man can and should avoid deaths in cases like this one. If Foster had been sober, there's a good possibility that he could have avoided hitting Judge Chase by veering or braking within a split second."

"If you charge him with Aggravated DUI," Norman said, "the jury is going to throw this case out. You can't win. Why not look beyond that thick prosecutor skin of yours and determine yourself that there is no case against Harry Foster except DUI."

"Maybe, maybe not. We'll see after I study the report. I will promise you that we'll move as quickly as we can on this. That's all I can give you for now."

Harry Foster was charged with Aggravated DUI resulting in a death, a felony that, if there were a conviction, would likely result in a sentence of three to fourteen years in prison. A jury would have to decide whether Harry's intoxication was the direct cause of Byron Chase's death. There was little doubt that a jury would find him guilty on the DUI charge. The immensely more important issue was how the jury would decide whether Harry could have avoided hitting Chase but for the fact that he was driving while drunk at what was determined to be a point fourteen BAC. Yes, he was well over the legal limit.

During the presentation of its case, the prosecutor proved the BAC percentage through extrapolation; police took a blood test within a few hours after the incident and got a point twelve. The evidence was hardly necessary since, even without extrapolation, it was clear that the BAC was already well over the legal limit at the time Foster struck Chase, but Garret was not leaving anything to chance. Typically, an extrapolation was not part of expert testimony unless the BAC was below the legal limit when the blood draw was completed sometimes hours later. Forensic evidence was presented to demonstrate that there were no skid marks approaching the exact location of Chase's body. Sergeant Kirk Olden testified as to his arrival at the accident scene after Harry placed a nine one one call. He related how emergency personnel had arrived immediately after; how Harry reeked of liquor on his breath, could not maintain his balance, and talked nervously; and how he put Harry under arrest.

Norman Caswell also relied on expert testimony. He proved that visibility was extremely limited, that there were no street lights, that there were dark clouds with no visible moon or stars, that it was impossible for Harry to see Chase or his car until Harry's car reached the down slope, and that from that point to where Chance was walking, there was less than one half of a second to react by braking.

In his final argument, Garret emphasized the effect of alcohol on Harry's ability to avoid hitting Byron Chase. "Clearly," he told the jury, "Foster's inebriated condition made it impossible for him to react to Bryon Chase walking alongside the road. If he hadn't been drinking and hadn't been well over the legal limit, he could have stopped or swerved to avoid hitting Byron Chase."

Norman pleaded his case. "The night was dark, the slope of the road allowed only a limited view of the immediate path of vision, and there was simply no time to take any action to avoid hitting Byron Chase. This was an accident that could not be prevented. There was no crime. This was an accident."

Judge John Blanchard instructed the jury that they could not presume guilt based on whether or not the defendant was intoxicated. They had to decide unanimously beyond a reasonable doubt that Harry Foster caused Byron Chase's death because of drunk driving.

The jury deliberated well into the evening before finally returning a verdict. When Judge Blanchard asked for the verdict, the jury foreman replied: "On the charge of Aggravated DUI, the jury finds the defendant Not Guilty. On the misdemeanor charge of Driving Under the Influence, we find the defendant Guilty as charged."

So, Norman Caswell won this one for his client. There would be a fine, license suspension, and supervision on the DUI but no prison time for taking a man's life. Did justice triumph in this case? Maybe.

One aspect of the case not heretofore mentioned was the drama going on outside of the courtroom. Mary Walton's job was to obtain necessary witnesses and look to the needs of victims' family members. That meant that she had to communicate with Mrs. Byron Chase. Mary's feelings of sympathy for the loss of the former judge along with her feelings of guilt in connection with her short-lived affair with him must have been somewhat transparent.

"You knew my husband quite well, didn't you?" Mrs. Chase said.

"Yes," Mary answered tentatively. "He was always very nice to me whenever I saw him in the courthouse."

"He was very nice to all attractive young women," the former judge's widow said. "We had a difficult relationship. After he retired, I thought that there was an opportunity for us to become closer, but it ended despite my prayers."

"I'm sure that he cared about you," Mary said. "He just needed time to adapt to the change from being on the Bench."

"Do you think so?" Mrs. Chase asked. "I don't. You see, even after he wasn't seeing anyone, as far as I could tell, I had a dream. St. Monica, patron of wives, appeared and told me that Byron was obsessed with a woman in the courthouse. Do you have any idea who that might have been?"

Chapter Twenty-Four

Only about forty-two per cent of car crashes are caused by drunk drivers. There are youthful and sometimes not so youthful reckless, negligent, or just plain stupid driving of various kinds, and distracted driving – people with their attention on something other than their driving. Text messaging is a growing problem and is illegal in some states. Use of a cell phone can be dangerous. Can you really always key in on your driving if you have your mind on your conversation while having only one hand on the steering wheel? There are numerous other distractions – fiddling with the radio or the CD player, chomping on a hamburger, setting a GPS, talking to others in the car (some drivers, always polite, turn completely around to establish eye contact with a back seat passenger), applying make-up, drinking pop, lighting up, checking out the cute blonde on the sidewalk, on and on. Then there is ROAD RAGE.

Elaine, Carrie, and Heather Sanford held on to hopes that their father would become a decent human being. All they knew was that at this point in his life, he had been guilty of domestic violence, perhaps sexual abuse, uncontrollable anger, lying, and cheating. Not a good resume for anyone. Heather had become a medical student and, perhaps not surprisingly, she hoped to become a psychiatrist. Long before she was qualified in that field, she did a practice run with Paul Sanford.

"Dad," she said, having invited him for dinner one evening, "we talk about you and wonder how you're doing. I know I told you to stay away from us, but it would be nice to have a father again. We all agree on that."

"That's a nice thought," Sanford said, "but I will always be your father. I've made some mistakes, but I've worked to rectify them."

"I know that your daughters haven't been communicating with you. We could start there."

"Heather, I really am a changed man. I just haven't had the opportunity to prove that to you and your sisters. Your mother, of course, is finished with me, but I would like to see the three of you once in a while."

"I know that this dinner invitation came out of the blue," Heather said, "but I've talked to Elaine and Carrie about each of us having you over for dinner once a month, at least we would like to see if that would work out for you and for us."

"That would be wonderful," Sanford said, "and maybe I could take all of you to dinner at a nice restaurant once in a while."

"That would be great ... You know, Dad, that settlement money came in between us some, but I want to reassure you that I still have funds if there is ever a need for money by Mom, Elaine, Carrie, or you. You know that, don't you?"

"I'm doing fine financially," Sanford responded. "I did go through a difficult time a few years back, but I'm on my feet. It's nice to know, though, that I could get some help from you if I needed it. I never thought I would have to beg from my daughter, but that's how it goes."

"You know I'm not talking about begging, Dad," Heather explained. "Please don't look at it that way."

"Okay, I won't. Anyway, thanks for inviting me over for dinner. I look forward to hearing from your sisters."

Paul Sanford may have been the consummate actor. He played the heartstrings of his daughters in an apparent attempt to reconcile while, consciously or subconsciously, he still had his eye on that pot of gold that was Heather's settlement share. After accepting several dinner invitations from each of his daughters, he invited all three to join him for dinner at one of Springfield's finest Italian restaurants, Saputo's. It was a Tuesday evening, and the restaurant was only half-full. Along with the scarcity of patrons came relative quiet, giving the four diners an opportunity to talk without shouting.

"Okay, all three of you have invited me to dinner, and I've enjoyed every one of them," Sanford said. "Order anything you want, the more expensive the better."

"Did you win the lottery?" Carrie said.

"Net yet. I do play. I play each of your birthday dates along with mine and your mother's, and then I throw in a lucky thirteen. It's a winner for sure any day now."

"Anyway, you're job is going well, isn't it?" Elaine asked. "So, you don't really need the lotto to be prosperous."

"No, no, not at all. No, my life is good and so much better now that I'm talking to the three of you."

Heather was still doubtful, based on what was determined when Henry Oswald reviewed her father's potential investments of her money. "I'm glad to hear that you're doing well, Dad."

"You all take good care of your mother, don't you?" Sanford asked half in jest but opening up an avenue that had been closed; they had not discussed their mother at the individual dinners.

"We see her quite a lot," Elaine reported. "You know, don't you, that she's been seeing someone?"

"Of course. She's been seeing what's-his-name," Sanford said.

"You don't really know, do you?" Carrie said.

"No," Sanford admitted.

"She met him at church," Carrie said. "I think that she was just bored at first. We were all getting so busy that she didn't see much of us."

"So what's this gallant knight do?" Sanford asked.

"We don't know too much about him. He was married once. His wife died. They didn't have any children."

"So, is he making big bucks or not?"

"He's a doctor, so I guess he has a good income," Carrie answered. "That's all I know about him."

"We weren't really going to bring it up," Elaine said, "but it has become serious. We should tell you that they're going to be getting married."

"Why in hell would she want to do that?" Sanford exploded.

"Dad," Heather said, "it's been about four years since the divorce. Maybe she's just lonely."

"When is the wedding?" Sanford asked and then, sarcastically, asked: "Is it going to be a big wedding, wedding gown, reception, hundreds of people?"

"It's scheduled for March, two months from today," Elaine said. "No, it's going to be a small, private ceremony with just a few friends."

"I guess I won't be invited," Sanford said.

"Please don't get upset about this, Dad," Heather said. "He's really a very nice man."

"As compared to her first husband, you mean," Sanford snapped. "I hope you all enjoy your meal. I'm afraid this news has put a bad taste in my mouth."

"Dad, please don't let this news spoil everything that we've all done in … reconciling," Heather pleaded.

"I just don't care any more," Sanford said. "Every time I'm down, somebody kicks me in the face … Look, I'm not hungry. I think I'm going to call it a night. Here's my credit card, Heather. Use it and give it back to me when I see you again."

"That's all right, Dad," Heather said. "Keep your card. I'll get the check. You can buy us dinner some other time, okay?"

"Sure, Heather, pick up the check. Why not? You've got plenty of the green stuff."

A hungry and dejected Paul Sanford stormed out of the restaurant without any goodbyes. When he reached his car in the parking lot, he kicked the side of the door, then opened and then slammed it closed after he was in the car. He pounded the steering wheel with the side of his fist a few times, and then he sat with his eyes closed for a few moments. Finally, he made his way out of the parking lot onto the two-lane road. There was a car approaching in his lane, but he was sure that there was ample time to move onto the road before that car arrived. The other driver didn't think so. He didn't like the idea of having to slow down for Sanford's entrance, so he leaned on the horn. The sound jarred Sanford's already jittery nervous system.

Sanford slowed down. What the hell is his hurry, he said to himself. Well, he's going to have to go even slower. Sanford slowed down to twenty-five in the forty-five mile an hour speed zone. Eat crow, Bastard, he thought. The driver behind him hit the horn again, hard and long, and Sanford slowed done to fifteen miles an hour. With traffic approaching in the other lane, the driver behind him had no opportunity to pass. Finally, he could pass, but, after he did, he slowed down to fifteen miles an hour, blocking Sanford's progress. A moment later, Sanford was able to pass the other driver. Then he slowed down to about ten miles an hour. After a minute or so of listening to the other driver blow his horn, Sanford pulled over to the side of the road. So did the other driver. Both drivers exited their vehicles and headed toward each other.

"What's your problem?" Sanford shouted.

"My problem is going to be your problem, you stupid son of a bitch," the other driver said.

Sanford stood inches away from the man but was not frightened. Although angry and threatening in his voice and manner, the other driver was a man with a slight build and wore horn-rimmed glasses. Easily, he could have passed for a clerk or a bookkeeper except for the way he was dressed. He wore pink pants and a salmon-colored shirt decorated with the imprints of roses. Sanford raised a forefinger and tapped the man on the chest.

"I don't have time for punks like you," Sanford said. "Stay off the road if you're going to act nuts every time you get behind the wheel."

The man looked down at Sanford's finger. "Don't do that!"

The veins in Sanford's neck bulged as though they were about to explode. He tapped the man with his finger twice more in succession. "Then, get out of my way!"

"I told you not to do that, you old fool," the salmon-colored shirt wearer said. "You're messing with the wrong guy."

"Look, you little jerk," Sanford said, "I've had a bad day. I don't need some idiot telling me what I can and can't do." Then he did it again: He poked the man in the chest, hard this time.

Sanford never saw it coming. With lightening speed, the other driver thrust a quickly opened switchblade into Sanford's ribs. Blood gushed from his body. He looked with amazement at his sudden wound. He didn't feel the incursion for a moment and then lost his ability to stand. Sanford crumpled into a heap there on the side of the road. He never recovered.

Chapter Twenty-Five

It was nothing but coincidence that Walter Caine and Billy Butler were released on the very same day from the Centralia prison. Warden Gary Watkins had high hopes for Walter; they had parted on good terms as virtual colleagues in the publishing of hundreds of articles that had influenced prosecutors, police, and the public, although there were still some who thought that the idea of a prisoner having access to outside communication was not right. As for Butler, the warden was simply happy to see him go. It's not that he caused problems; the warden just never trusted him. He thought that Butler's heroic action in saving Walter's life was more a desire to get in on the action than an impulse to do something decent for a fellow human being.

Once Ed and Betty Caine assumed custody of Johnny, they told him the truth about his father in a way that Johnny understood that this father made a major mistake and was repaying society by serving time. He also learned about his father's columns and how they had benefited so many. He read the articles as soon as he was old enough to understand them, and he visited his father along with his grandparents at least once a month.

Consequently, the ground was laid for Walter to become a father again. It would also now be possible to put the crash and its aftermath behind him. Harry Foster, now with a better understanding of Walter's difficulties because of his own drunk driving accusation and trial, even gave Walter a job back at Foster Ford. The employees who worked there at the time of the crash, especially those who were at Friday's that fated night, were certainly uneasy in the beginning, but they, too, were so impressed with Walter's work ethic and his willingness to speak openly about the incident that put him in prison that within a few months they were at ease again. But Walter himself still did not feel restored. That's when he contacted Americans Against Intoxicated Drivers.

Much to his amazement, Jack Northrup did not succeed in his efforts to have the crash victims' families share the settlement money in significant amounts. Although Walter had an unusual request, Northrup was always willing to consider the potential of a possible opportunity to raise funds.

One source of income for AAID was an outreach called Victim Impact Panels. These are offered by a variety of organizations – the Red Cross, State's Attorneys' offices, Probation Departments, Victim Impact Speakers, and Mothers Against Drunk Driving, as well as AAID. The VIPs are presented to first-time DUI offenders with attendance required by the court as part of the sentence or as a condition of probation. Victims of drunk driving crashes appear on these panels to talk about their very personal losses caused by a drunk driver. Typically, the panelist is someone who was seriously injured or someone who lost a member of the family. The purpose is to put an image in the minds of attendees that something much worse could have happened to them than being cited for DUI; they could have killed someone or could have been killed themselves. These panels have proven to help prevent recidivism. After attending a VIP, a first-time DUI offender gives serious thought to never driving drunk again. The offender has to pay a fee to attend the session.

While the other organizations offered VIPs solely to accomplish the purpose of discouraging recidivism, AAID saw it as an opportunity to produce income for the organization that would help to pay those inflated salaries in the national office. Consequently, after a number of local courts agreed to allow AAID to offer the panels, AAID began a process of gouging the offenders while maintaining a policy of not paying the panelists for their participation.

The victims were very effective in their participation. In evaluations, virtually every attendee reported that the panels were beneficial to them, that the attendee was very unlikely to continue to drink and drive as a result of the panel's message, and that the single best reason not to drink and drive was that the attendee could hurt or kill someone. Panelists were victims, thus the name Victim Impact Panel. Nevertheless, Northrup was intrigued with the idea proposed by Walter Caine, which was the subject of a discussion long ago with Norman Caswell. Walter wanted to continue his retribution through participation as a panelist.

"We are interested in your participating in the panels, Mr. Caine," Northrup said upon arriving in Walter's office from Dallas.

"Good," Walter said. "I know that it is the usual practice to have only victims on the panels, but I thought that my participation could be effective. After all, I'm the epitome of why people should not drink and drive."

"I've read your columns with great interest," Northrup said. "I'm confident that you will be a very powerful speaker, but we want to go much beyond that level."

"I don't understand," Walter said.

"We want you to come to work for us as a full-time speaker. We would gain recognition for you through the Victim Impact Panels, but our very immediate goal would be to have you speak at fund raising meetings of our state chapters and for significant fees at corporate meetings and for college groups."

"You actually believe that you could bring in considerable income in that way?" Walter asked.

"Yes, and we would pay you handsomely, say $200,000 a year."

"Wouldn't that be inconsistent with the purpose of raising funds? Would I even bring in $200,000 with my appearances?"

"We think so. We have never shied away from compensating our employees well to accomplish our goals. Of course, you will have to agree to speak for us exclusively, and you would have to sign a non-compete clause prohibiting you from appearing as a speaker ever again when and if you leave AAID."

"Is that legal?"

"We'll have our attorneys put it in a form that assures its legality."

"I'm overwhelmed," Walter said.

"Also, we would want to hire you as an independent contractor. There might be objections by some members to putting an offender on our payroll."

"And that's legal also?" Walter could not help but ask.

"Oh, yes," Northrup answered. "We'll have our lawyers structure it so it fits IRS guidelines."

"All of this is very flattering," Walter said, "but it just sounds shady to me. It doesn't feel right."

"Look beyond how your gut feels," Northrup advised. "Just think of two considerations: one, you'll influence people, and two, you'll raise a lot of money for our organization, money that will do some good."

"Some good, such as paying me a salary of $200,000."

"If that's not enough, we might be able to work out some bonus deals also," Northrup told Walter.

Walter was silent for a moment. Obviously, he was weighing and measuring Northrup's offer. "I'll have to think about it. Give me a few weeks. There's someone I want to consult before I agree to work with you."

The idea of speaking to the public and to AAID members in order to raise money didn't set quite right with Walter. The original plan, the one suggested by Norman Caswell almost nine years ago, speaking at Victim Impact Panels, made the most sense to him. Being paid $200,000, maybe even bonuses above that figure, didn't seem quite right when his primary qualification for earning this kind of money was that he was responsible for deaths and injuries. Before he made any decision to participate in any way, he wanted to talk to the man whose compassion probably turned his life around: Reverend Bill Goodwin. It took some courage to do so, but he placed a call to the Goodwins and asked them if he could come to visit them. The Goodwins agreed to allow the visit, without hesitation.

"I know that this is unusual, visiting parents of a young woman who is no longer alive because of my acts," Caine began.

"I would say that it is extremely unusual," Mary said. "However, we agreed to your visit because we have read your columns while you were in prison, and we are convinced that you are genuine."

"And," Bill Goodwin said, "I was convinced of your remorse at the Sentencing Hearing. There is such a thing as forgiveness, you know."

"Yes, and that's exactly why I have come to see you. You see, I have dedicated my life in a surely vain attempt to expunge my wrong. I know I never can, but I want to try. The articles were only a small beginning."

"Mr. Caine, I am a dying man. Soon, it will be over for me, but, as you well know, I do have faith in an after life and eternity. The imminence of my transition from life to beyond gives me, I think, an almost hindsight view of this world. In short, I believe in your sincerity. What is it that you need?"

"I'm sorry, young man," Mary said. "He always talks like that. He is, after all, a minister. He could have simply asked why you came here."

"I am being asked to become a panelist to convince DUI offenders that they should never drink and drive. In addition, I am being requested to make speaking appearances to raise money for the operation of Americans Against Intoxicated Drivers."

"And you have some reluctance to do these things?" Mary asked.

"Exactly. It is as though I would be using the deaths of your daughter and the other young women in the crash to provide some questionable benefit. I will participate to the extent that you advise and to that extent only. I think I owe you that."

Jack Northrup's direct line sprang to life in his office in Dallas. He had been told that the answer from Walter Caine was forthcoming.

"This is Jack Northrup."

"Walter Caine. I won't be coming to work for AAID."

"I'm very sorry to hear that, Walter, and I'm surprised," Northrup said. "If it's a matter of money …"

"No," Walter said, "it's a matter of honor and decency. I intend to volunteer to assist organizations such as Mothers Against Drunk Driving or Victim Impact Speakers in their Victim Impact Panels. I think that I can have some influence on individuals who have made my mistake by telling them what the consequences are, including prison and never really living with themselves again. I have the encouragement in this from the Goodwins, the Fergusons, and Heather Sanford. I visited with all of them. Then, I saw Henry Oswald who did me the additional favor of sharing information about your organization."

"Wait a minute!" Northrup ordered. "I gave Oswald confidential information. You mean he shared that with you?"

"He shared with me the fact that your staff in Dallas is grossly overpaid while you provide a minimum of services, all accomplished by volunteers or poorly paid dedicated employees in state chapters."

"Don't be foolish, Walter," Northrup said. "You can make a lot of money working with us."

"Mr. Northrup, I am going to dedicate the rest of my life to honor those who were victimized by me. Those plans do not include working with Americans Against Intoxicated Drivers."

The State's Attorney's office in Madison County presented Victim Impact Panels every month. This county needed that many VIPs because DUIs were rampant. The Illinois Secretary of State's pamphlet called DUI Facts reported that there were 1,386 DUI arrests in the county in the prior year. That wasn't the worst of it. In addition to those charged with DUI, a misdemeanor, there were thirty drivers charged with Aggravated DUI: sixteen because they had several prior DUIs or were driving on a suspended license when they were caught drunk on the road, six because they had caused a serious injury, and eight because the drivers had taken at least one life in a crash. There were no arrests for a few other drunk drivers, not charged because they killed themselves in the crashes. The Assistant State's Attorney who monitored the panels asked Walter to participate as a panelist.

Joining Walter for the Victim Impact Panel were Katie who lost her daughter and granddaughter in a crash caused by a drunk driver and Helen whose six-year-old daughter was killed when Helen's ex-husband, who had visiting rights, could not handle the car because of his high BAC combined with drugs in his system. The car left the road, struck a tree, and was the dangerous weapon that took the life of his passenger, his daughter.

Each of the women told their very personal tragic story. Each could not help but shed tears as they related how the deaths occurred, how they were notified of the crashes, and how their lives were so drastically changed as a result.

Walter began by telling the audience of first-time DUI offenders about all of the circumstances that led to his entering the highway on the exit instead of the entrance, how he struck the Howard Christian College students with violent force that killed three of the students and forced a fourth student to go through unimaginable trauma and pain. Then, he ended his statement: "Incredibly, the parents of the students I killed have told me that they forgive me. I will never forgive myself. Three young women who deserved to have long, happy lives never had that opportunity because of me. That is something that I live with everyday. I think about it, cry about it, and regret it every one of those days.

"Please don't repeat my mistakes. There is blood on my hands because I drank and drove. I had a choice. I didn't have to get into my car that night after drinking for hours. I didn't have to enter the wrong side of the highway and cause a crash that resulted in so much misery, and I didn't have to spend eight and a half years away from my family in prison, but I did all those things because I drank and drove. Don't do it."

Victim Impact Speakers, one of the organizations active in presenting Victim Impact Panels, also had two familiar names as speakers: Mary and Bill Goodwin. While Bill was sometimes difficult to hear, his emotional presentations were very effective. Mary was impressive. She captured the attention, the sympathies, and the hearts of audiences, no matter how tough. They never appeared on the same panel as Walter, but their participation came to the attention of AAID. Even though the Goodwins had opted against the hundred thousand to several hundred thousand dollar contribution suggested by Northrup, they had decided that the organization's goals were worthwhile, and they did offer contributions both of money and participation. Northrup saw an opening to assure additional contributions from them. He suggested that Mary become a member of AAID's Board of Directors. Mary agreed to serve.

Within a year, Mary's participation resulted in influencing other Board members to work diligently on their responsibilities as Board members, not continue to be motionless rubber stamps for the ideas and actions of their energetic and often persuasive Executive Director. This led to an unexpected result for Jack Northrup.

"Jack, you know," Mary said, "the Board met in executive session a few days ago to review staff salaries."

"I don't think that salaries should be increased at this time," Northrup volunteered.

"No, we don't either. We looked at the entire financial situation and have deliberated budget cuts."

"I'm happy to stay at my present salary for the time being, if that helps," Northrup said.

"My colleagues on the Board have taken a hard look at our operation," Mary said. "As a result, virtually all salaries with the exception of yours are to be cut in half. If there are affected employees who are unwilling to accept the salary reductions, they will be replaced."

"That may be a problem. It won't be easy to replace some of the expertise we have available to us now."

Mary nodded her head slightly. "We have a comprehensive report that was voluntarily submitted to us from staff member Don Dolittle. He agrees with our assessment."

Northrup was stunned at this disclosure. "I don't think that you should believe anything he says. Actually I've been thinking of replacing him."

"That will no longer be an option for you," Mary said. "The Board members made one other significant decision. As Donald Trump would say, Mr. Northrup, you're fired."

Chapter Twenty-Six

Wild man Billy Butler was free, free, free. For a short period, he returned to Peoria. He managed to get a job selling health insurance. The company had some concern about his background, but his outgoing, persuasive manner convinced the boss to put him on the payroll. Actually, he was quite good at the job with one small exception: He spent every spare moment he could find at the gambling casinos. He also spent some time, not much, inquiring into the whereabouts of Mary Butler. Finally, he did get a lead. A friend of a friend thought that he had heard that Mary moved downstate, Springfield, he thought.

The boss said why not, the company could use a good salesman in the Springfield office. Butler had a solid idea on how to find Mary in Springfield. She worked in the Circuit Court Clerk's office in Peoria. He surmised correctly that she would look for employment somewhere at the courthouse in Springfield. Assuming that her job, whatever it was, would have a quitting time somewhere between four and six in the afternoon, he took up his watch at a bus stop bench just across from the courthouse. Imagine Mary's surprise to see her ex-husband as she approached the parking lot.

"Nice to see you again, Mary," Butler said.

"Billy? It's you, isn't it? What are you doing here?"

"I wanted to see you, Sweetie. I missed you."

"What are you talking about?" Mary said. "I don't even know you. I haven't seen you in over ten years. I wasn't sure whether you were even alive."

"Well, Babe, I've been out of touch, you might say," Billy said. "Let's have some coffee or a drink and catch up."

"Billy," Mary responded, "I'm not interested in having anything to do with you. Since our divorce, I've put you totally out of my mind."

"Divorce? What do you mean, divorce? You're my wife."

"Not any more, Billy, not since you didn't appear in court after deserting me. I have a new life now, and you're not any part of it."

"Whoa," Butler said. "You're not the shy, unassuming young woman you used to be, are you?"

"No, I'm not, Billy. I'm not the same person, and I'm certainly not your wife. Please just go away; I don't want to have anything to do with you."

"Do we have to stand here like this? At least give me a chance to talk to you."

Mary was understandably confused as to what she should do. She was still in shock from Butler's sudden appearance, but her sense of fairness prevailed.

"I suppose you're entitled to that," Mary relented. "I'll meet you at Steak N' Shake at eight tomorrow morning. That's the best I can do."

Walter Caine was not so difficult to find. Ed Caine was in the phone book, and Walter and Johnny were still living with Walter's parents. Walter was not particularly pleased to hear from his old fellow prisoner, but he concealed his true feelings, still indebted to Billy for his quick action in cutting down Bull on his way to dispensing serious mayhem on Walter's body. They agreed to meet at a local sports bar.

"Didn't think I'd be seeing you again," Walter said.

"I thought I'd drop in and see how you're doing, Buddy," Butler said.

"I'm doing great. It's good to be out in the real world again," Walter commented. "I'm doing exactly what I want to do now with my life. How about you? Have a job?"

"Sure, I'm a super salesman, but I'm not having all that much fun. Where are the women in this burg?"

"You're asking the wrong guy," Walter said. "I don't go out much. You're on your own in that department."

"I do know one woman in Springfield. I'm meeting her in the morning. She's my ex-wife, believe it or not."

"I didn't know you were the marrying kind," Walter said.

"Nah, I'm not, really," Butler answered. "It was a short marriage, but she's here, and she owes me."

"Billy," Walter said, "that's exactly the attitude that's going to get you back in the big house. Why don't you just let it go?"

"Yeah, maybe you're right. Anyway, the real reason I'm here is to tell you that we never properly celebrated our release. I'll even buy."

It was difficult to turn down Butler's invitation, not because Butler offered to buy, not because Walter needed to celebrate, but only because it's difficult to reject a man who probably saved your life when all he's asking is to get together for a few drinks. "I don't drink, Billy. I've put that behind me also."

"So I'll drink alcohol while you drink Diet Pepsi. It's no big deal. How about tomorrow night at a sports bar I found just east of town? We'll shoot a few darts, watch some baseball on the tube. I'll even pick you up."

"Okay," Walter finally agreed, "but if you're drinking, I'm doing the driving back home."

Tom Lansing enjoyed having breakfast at Steak N' Shake a few times a week on his way to the office or an early court appearance. It wasn't the most popular breakfast place in Springfield. The restaurant was typically busy for lunch or dinner but had only a sparse breakfast following. However, Tom liked the prompt service and the waitress who always served him and remembered what he typically ordered, two scrambled eggs, two sausage links, hash brown potatoes, and coffee with two creams, no sugar. When he looked up briefly from his newspaper, he saw a somewhat familiar face. He didn't place her at first, but then he realized that she was the victim/witness coordinator in the State's Attorney's office, so he waved back at her and returned to The State Journal-Register.

 A minute or two after sitting in a booth, she was joined by her ex-husband.

 "Look," she said peremptorily, "I don't know why you're here, but I'm married. You should know that. Our divorce was final over ten years ago."

 "Married? How can that be? I never agreed to a divorce."

 "I guess you don't understand the law, then. You deserted me. There was a hearing. You did not make an appearance. I was granted the divorce. That's all there was to it."

 "Look, Baby," Butler said, "If that's the way it is, then I guess I'll have to go to court to see what I can do about that. I think the divorce wasn't legal because I never got notice. You've committed bigamy, Babe."

 "You should also know that my husband is the State's Attorney. I think he knows the law quite well … And stop calling me Babe. I'm not your Babe."

 "I'll tell you what, Cookie," Butler said, "I have no problem with your sloughing me off. I'm making money, and I'm out of prison."

 "You were in prison?"

 "That's it. Armed robbery, but now I'm bringing in bucks and I'm on the loose."

 "I just realized that you've been drinking," Mary said. "I can smell the alcohol all the way over here. It's eight o'clock in the morning!"

 "And I've just begun, Babe, I mean Cookie. Look, don't sweat it. I'm out of here. You can pick up the check for my coffee. Wait a minute! How about one little kiss for old time's sake?"

 "Don't be ridiculous," Mary said, clearly alarmed.

Butler came around to her side of the booth and sat next to her. "Come on, it won't hurt you."

As Butler held her by the shoulders, moving her toward him, a large hand came down quickly and forcefully on Butler's shoulder. "I think I overheard an objection from the lady," Tom Lansing said. "Maybe you'd better just move along."

"You think that you can make me, Buster?" Butler sneered.

"I believe that I can," Tom said.

Just then, Tom's friends at the restaurant, the cashier, the waitress, the somewhat large bus guy with the biceps and the tattoos, all stood around him.

"I believe everyone here wants me to leave," Butler said.

Chapter Twenty-Seven

But for the crash, Patti Goodwin, Maris Oswald, and Cayla Ferguson might have lived a long, happy life. Who knows what they would have done with the fifty or sixty or seventy years that they should have had in front of them? All three were bright, energetic, caring young women who might have accomplished about anything. They might also have had children and grandchildren who might have contributed to mankind in some way. But for the crash, Heather Sanford could not have had the inspiration or the finances to attend medical school, but, then, she never would have had to suffer the trauma and the injuries caused by the crash. But for the crash, Walter Caine might have lived a productive life without ever seeing the inside of a prison; he proved to be a decent man, despite causing the tragedy. Of course, but for the crash, he never would have contributed his writings that were so influential.

But for the crash, Paul Sanford's marriage may have survived, and he may have survived. But for the crash, the Oswalds may not have forged into such a tightly knit family that one daughter was able to go on to medical school, and Henry Oswald might not have been in a position to save Heather Sanford's settlement fund. But for the crash, the Fergusons very likely would have remained divorced; the tragedy brought them back together after twenty years.

But for the crash, Reverend Bill Goodwin might never have found that his capacity for forgiveness was unmatched, despite his suffering from a body racked with Parkinson's, and Mary Goodwin may not have saved Americans Against Intoxicated Drivers from the lack of wisdom demonstrated by its Executive Director.

But for the crash, Norman Caswell may never have had a client who was truly remorseful for his actions, a client so much different than his usual clients who regretted vicious crimes only because they were caught and sent to prison. But for the crash, Tom Lansing would not have had the opportunity to do so much good for four families by out-negotiating a powerful insurance company lawyer, even though it is certainly true that all the money in the world could not truly compensate them for their losses and their suffering.

But for the crash, John Blanchard would not have been eased out of his job as State's Attorney, and Byron Chase would not have left the Bench under pressure and then died never having removed those pressures, both because the sentence meted out to Walter Caine was insufficient in the minds of many. And without that, John Blanchard would not have become a judge and Garret Nelson would not have become a State's Attorney, or at least neither of these developments would have occurred quite so soon.

But for the crash, Bull, prisoner No. 5416, may have survived his prison term because he would not have attacked Walter Caine but for Caine being in prison as one result of the crash. But for the same reason, Billy Butler would never have known Walter Caine with consequences still to come.

But for the crash and the intricacies involving the prosecution of Walter Caine, Mary Walters may never have grown to love and wed Garret Nelson.

But for the crash, Americans Against Intoxicated Drivers may have not sunk to such enormous lows in their fund-raising endeavors.

By the time Billy Butler honked his car horn in front of Walter Caine's home, he was very intoxicated; he had been drinking all day beginning before his brief meeting with Mary Walton, now Nelson, and his expulsion from Steak N' Shake. Walter, of course, was not aware of Butler's condition until he was in the vehicle and Butler sped away from the curb.

"Hey, slow down," Walter said. "There's no hurry to get there, is there?"

"I'm ready to celebrate, man," Butler said. "Yahoo!"

"What's going on? Watch where you're going!"

"Just hang on, old buddy. You're in for the ride of your life."

"Have you been drinking already?" Walter asked, now alarmed.

"You bet I have," Butler answered.

"Stop the car, Billy. Stop the car now!"

"Ah, the man with all the goody-goody advice is spooked. Don't sweat it! I can drive this baby like nobody you've ever seen."

"Billy, stop being stupid. Stop the car, damn it!"

"Watch this move, Wally, passing three cars all at once, zoom, zoom."

"Slow down! This is crazy. Please slow down and stop, Billy. Don't do this."

Butler succeeded in passing the three cars on the two-lane road but stayed in the passing lane too long. A car in the lane was heading straight at them. Walter reached over and jerked the wheel to the right as Butler hit the brakes. The car careened off the road and down an embankment, flipping over and over. When the car came to rest, it burst into flames. Neither the driver nor the passenger survived.

But for the tragic crash between drunk driver Walter Caine and four Howard Christian College students almost ten years before, Walter Caine would not have been sent to prison and would not have ever had contact with a man who saved his life and then took his life.

Does the justice system work? Not always, but sometimes true justice comes outside the courtroom. Drunk, reckless, distracted, and stupid drivers will continue to exist despite laws and other efforts to prevent their consequences. For Walter, a man who meant no harm to anyone and then attempted to do all he could to make up for killing those young women and injuring another, his life ended in yet one more senseless crash.

It is certainly true that every act, positive or negative, has consequences not only on the actor but sometimes on a reverberating number of others. It is not enough for an individual to be concerned with how his or her behavior impacts that person's physical and mental well-being; there has to be serious consideration always of the ever widening joy or sadness that can be brought about by a single act.

Every drunk driver who has attended or will ever attend a Victim Impact Panel believes that he has been duly punished with an embarrassing arrest, a fine, and the suspension of a driver's license. It could have been much, much worse. If Walter Caine had been stopped by a police officer before he entered the highway at the exit instead of the entrance that night, he, too, would have believed that he was receiving an adequate penalty by being treated exactly the same as other arrested drunk drivers, but he was not arrested that night before he got on the highway, and the wildfire that he caused swept through the lives of many, just the way that all we do that is good or evil forever touches others. It's our choice.

THE END